For more than forty years,
Yearling has been the leading name
in classic and award-winning literature
for young readers.

Yearling books feature children's
favorite authors and characters,
providing dynamic stories of adventure,
humor, history, mystery, and fantasy.

Trust Yearling paperbacks to entertain,
inspire, and promote the love of reading
in all children.

OTHER YEARLING BOOKS YOU WILL ENJOY

THE TRIAL, *Jen Bryant*

PIECES OF GEORGIA, *Jen Bryant*

CROOKED RIVER, *Shelley Pearsall*

TROUBLE DON'T LAST, *Shelley Pearsall*

BELLE PRATER'S BOY, *Ruth White*

UNDER THE WATSONS' PORCH, *Susan Shreve*

THE LEGACY OF GLORIA RUSSELL, *Sheri Gilbert*

STEALING FREEDOM, *Elisa Carbone*

STORM WARRIORS, *Elisa Carbone*

RINGSIDE

1925

VIEWS FROM THE SCOPES TRIAL

a novel

JEN BRYANT

A YEARLING BOOK

This is a work of fiction. All incidents and dialogue, and all characters with the exception of some well-known historical and public figures, are products of the author's imagination and are not to be construed as real. Where real-life historical and public figures appear, the situations, incidents, and dialogues concerning those persons are largely fictional and are not intended to depict actual events or to change the largely fictional nature of the work. In all other respects, any resemblance to persons living or dead is entirely coincidental.

 Published in the United States by Yearling, an imprint of Random House Children's Books, a division of Random House, Inc., New York. Originally published in hardcover by Alfred A. Knopf Books for Young Readers, New York, in 2008.

The Library of Congress has cataloged the hardcover edition of this work as follows:
Bryant, Jennifer.
Ringside, 1925 : views from the Scopes trial / Jen Bryant.
p. cm.
Summary: Visitors, spectators, and residents of Dayton, Tennessee, in 1925 describe, in a series of free-verse poems, the Scopes "monkey trial" and its effects on that small town and its citizens.
ISBN 978-0-375-84047-0 (trade) — ISBN 978-0-375-94047-7 (lib. bdg.)
1. Scopes, John Thomas—Trials, litigation, etc.—Juvenile fiction. 2. Evolution (Biology)—Study and teaching—Law and legislation—Tennessee—Juvenile fiction. [1. Scopes, John Thomas—Trials, litigation, etc.—Fiction. 2. Evolution—Study and teaching—Law and legislation—Fiction. 3. Community life—Fiction. 4. Dayton (Tenn.)—History—20th century—Fiction. 5. Novels in verse.] I. Title. II. Title: Ringside, nineteen twenty-five.
PZ7.5.B792Rin 2008
[Fic]—dc22
2007007177

ISBN: 978-0-440-42189-4 (pbk.)
Printed in the United States of America
10 9 8 7 6 5 4 3 2 1
First Yearling Edition

In memory of Mildred Oaks
(1909–2007)

Behold, I am doing a new thing;
now it springs forth, do you not
perceive it?

—Isaiah 43:19

Narrators in *Ringside, 1925*, in the order in which they appear:

PETER SYKES

Student at Rhea County High and an employee of Robinson's Drugs

WILLY AMOS

Twelve-year-old resident of Dayton who helps his father, a handyman

JIMMY LEE DAVIS

Student at Rhea County High, employee of Robinson's Drugs, and friend to Peter Sykes

MARYBETH DODD

Student at Rhea County High, lives with her widowed father, and works at the Mansion, a boardinghouse

TILLIE STACKHOUSE

Manager of the Mansion and cousin to Marybeth's father, Frank

BETTY BARKER

Resident of Dayton and member of the ladies' Bible study group

CONSTABLE FRAYBEL

Local law enforcement agent

ERNEST McMANUS

Methodist minister who has traveled to Dayton to view the trial

PAUL LEBRUN

Young reporter from the *St. Louis Post-Dispatch*, in town to cover the trial

PART 1

Why did [the State of Tennessee] pass the act? They passed it because they wanted to prohibit teaching in the public schools . . . a theory that man was descended from a lower order of animals. . . . [W]hen you teach that . . . you have taught a theory that denies God's Bible.

—Thomas Stewart, attorney general for the State of Tennessee

[A]re the teachers and scientists of this country in a [plot] to destroy the morals of the children to whom they have dedicated their lives? Are preachers the only ones in America who care about our youth? Is the church the only source of morality in this country?

—Dudley Malone, defense lawyer

PETER SYKES

That morning, Jimmy and me had hiked
clear to Connor's Pond, halfway up the mountain,
and back again. I hooked four bass

and three brown trout. Jimmy, who loves fishing
more than just about anything, caught
a dozen bluegills and a huge catfish his mother

promised to fry us for dinner. Soon as we got
back, we stashed our poles under the porch
and ran to Robinson's store for root beer floats.

We were sitting at the soda fountain,
sucking on our straws and listening to
Gershwin's "Rhapsody in Blue" on the radio,

when Mr. Walter White asked: "You boys seen
Mr. Scopes?" With school being out and it being
summer, we figured the new science teacher

must be in trouble. But Mr. White is our
school superintendent, so we figured
we'd be in bigger trouble if we didn't tell.

"We saw him a half hour ago," I said,
"heading over to the school."
"Dressed for tennis," Jimmy added.

He hurried back to the table where
Mr. Robinson and Mr. Rappleyea waited.
Then the Hicks brothers, both Dayton lawyers,

showed up in their jalopy
and all five of them jabbered
like magpies at a picnic.

WILLY AMOS

Those big ol' houses at the edge of town . . .
Pa says they were once grand and beautiful.
Now they're mostly heaps of bricks,
wood planks, broken glass. Some got
trees growin' right out the roofs, vines
twistin' out the doorways.

Pa says back before I was born, when the mines
were open and the furnaces made metal
for the railroads and tall city buildin's,
white families lived there—
"lace curtains in the windows, easy chairs
an' daisies on the porches in summer," Pa says.

Well, that sure ain't how it looks *this* summer.
There's skunks in the cellar,
bats in the attic,
mice in the kitchen sink.

When I'm not helpin' Pa, I come here
to root through the hallways and closets,
searchin' for somethin' I might be able
to fix up and sell—a flower vase,
a tin box, a watch face left behind
when those families moved to places
where jobs come easier.

'Most every year
the town council changes the number
on the little wooden sign
sayin' how many folks live here:
3,000, 2,600, 2,100, . . . and last year 1,800.

Pa and me, we don't got much need
for big numbers. I'm not sure what they mean,
'ceptin' I know that the first one

is biggest and the last one is smallest
and that means people are leavin'.

Twelve. Now that's a number I'm used to.
I was born here twelve years back:
May 1913. I ain't never lived anyplace
but Dayton, Tennessee,
so that last number
still seems like *plenty* of folks to me.

But maybe someday, if I move to a big city
like New Orleans, Chicago, or Detroit,
get me a steady job,
I'll live near even more people,
and a lot fewer
mice and skunks.

JIMMY LEE DAVIS

Tarnation! Poor Mr. Scopes!
He didn't know why
Mr. White came
to fetch him from
his tennis game

& bring him into Robinson's.
Me & Pete sipped
our sodas & listened
as he confessed
that back in the spring
when we were still in school,
he assigned us
the chapter on evolution,
which explained how
all the animals on earth
had started as simpler creatures
millions of years ago,
& how, over time,
they changed & developed
into the insects, birds,
fish, & mammals
we see today,
& how, even now,
they were still changing.
(I try not to think of
fish as my ancestors
when I'm cleaning them.)

Mr. Robinson held up a copy
of Hunter's *Civic Biology*,
which is the book we used
in school, which is also
one of the books he sells
in his store, & asked:

"Did you use this in class?"
Calm as Connor's Pond,
Mr. Scopes said: "Sure I did, Fred.
You can't teach science
at Rhea County High
without using that book!"

Mr. Robinson smiled
wide as a catfish unhooked.
"Well, John, the American
Civil Liberties Union will pay
to defend the first person
who challenges the new law
against teaching evolution
in Tennessee. So we were
wondering if you'd mind
being arrested, to get
the whole business
right out on the table,
right here in Dayton."

Lordy! My ears
were burnin' & Pete near
choked to death
on his root beer.
Mr. Scopes saw us eaves-
dropping. He winked &
tipped his cap. "Sure, I guess
that'd be all right—
long as I can finish

my tennis match."
The men took turns
patting him on the back,
thanking him, telling him
not to worry; they'd send
someone down to
arrest him
later that afternoon.

PETER SYKES

I helped Marybeth Dodd with her groceries
and told her about Mr. Scopes. "Poor man,"
she said. "If he's a criminal, then I'm Babe Ruth."

We both laughed at the thought of that.
"Thanks a lot, Pete," she said, her smile flashing
in the sunlight. "Anytime, Marybeth," I said,

feeling the color rise in my cheeks. I quick
pedaled to the end of her street so she
didn't see. (What's gotten into me?)

Turning the corner, I rode fast and hard
across the tracks, up the hill, till
there were no more stores and houses,

just the farms spread out on either side,
like patchwork blankets as far as I could see.
I pedaled faster. Just about the time my thighs ached

and I needed a break, I came to the big oak
at the foot of Walton's Ridge. I leaned the bike
against the trunk, laced my shoes on tight, hiked

the steep dirt path made by the Cherokee
before there even *was* a Tennessee. At the top,
there's a flat rock called Buzzard Point, where you

can stand and look out over the Tennessee River Valley,
watch the steam rise from the Southern Railway line
as it snakes its way from one end to the other.

Used to be, I'd climb up there to dream about
my future . . . running my own hardware store,
settling down with someone from school.

But I'll be a senior next year and now
I'm not so sure. Ever since we studied geology
I can't stop reading about rocks. I've read

every book in our library and sent away for more,
and I like each one better than the one before.
Volcanoes, earthquakes, erosion, and carbonates—

who'd think they'd be exciting? (But they are.)
Some nights I fall asleep reciting
the scientific names of minerals and gems.

Now my dream is to ride in an airplane
through the Rocky Mountains . . . to see for myself
the layers of sediment built up over centuries,

and those places where the earth's crust broke
open, pushed up miles of new peaks.
Our state lawmakers passed the Butler Act

because they think science will poison our minds.
Well, I don't feel poisoned. I still believe in the divine.
Why should a bigger mind need a smaller God?

It's still a miracle how everything works,
how everything has a purpose. Even the buzzards
are beautiful in their own way. I watch them

steer from one invisible layer to another—
wings wide, using their tails as rudders—
searching for something my human eyes

can't find. When I flatten my back
against the rock and look up, a flock
of dark crosses blesses the Tennessee sky.

MARYBETH DODD

Mr. Scopes has been arrested.

Our brand-new (and handsome, too!)
math and general science teacher
has been arrested for breaking
the just-passed Butler Act of Tennessee,
which, according to Daddy's morning paper,
makes it illegal

> "to teach any theory that denies the story
> of the Divine Creation of man
> as taught in the Bible,
> and to teach instead that man has descended
> from a lower order of animals."

Pete Sykes was pedaling his bike
down Market Street, heading up toward
Buzzard Point. He stopped when he saw me,
helped me carry groceries.
(That was real sweet.)

Pete says it's not a real arrest—
they didn't use handcuffs or throw Mr. Scopes in jail—
it's mostly just paperwork. Still,
it appears there will be
a real honest-to-goodness trial,
right here in Dayton.

I mentioned it to Daddy this evening
while we were picking strawberries
from our one good patch,
and he said, "You see, Marybeth?
It just doesn't do to mess
with the Lord's word, to think
that some new scientific idea
can replace the Holy Book!"

"Daddy," I said, mixing my pick
of berries in the basket with his,
"I really don't think Mr. Scopes had any
intention of replacing the Holy Book.
I think he just wanted to teach science,
which is not the same as religion,
and I think what everyone at Rhea County High
likes about Mr. Scopes
is that he trusts us to learn both
and know the difference."

Daddy got quiet after that, though I could
hear him mumbling something
under his breath.

I started separating the bigger, sweeter berries
from the smaller, sour ones, until Daddy said:
"Leave 'em together, Marybeth—
if you use both, it makes a better jam."

I did as he said, but I swear
I heard the Lord himself
laughing.

TILLIE STACKHOUSE

The boardinghouse business has been slow,
so I've been writing to my sister, Lila, a history teacher
at a private school in New York City.
My husband did not like Lila much,
so after we got married and moved south,
we fell out of touch.

Then about ten years ago—
right after my A.J. died—
we started writing again. Now we exchange long letters
and samples of our favorite cookie recipes
regularly.

In my latest letter, I told Lila
how our state legislature
had recently passed the Butler Act, making it
illegal
for any public school educator

to give instruction on Charles Darwin's
theory of evolution
or to teach that man descended
from a lower order of animals.

I told Lila how five local men—
Fred Robinson, George Rappleyea, Walter White,
and the two Hicks brothers—
had gotten J. T. Scopes arrested,
so they could bring the evolution trial,
and hopefully lots of tourists,
to Dayton.

Lila's always been a big reader.
So I asked if she had ever studied Darwin
or read about his trip
on the HMS *Beagle* to the Galápagos Islands,
where he spent several years observing
the different animal species
and where he found the evidence he needed
to support his idea of "natural selection."

I told Lila how I'd read an article about it
in my *National Geographic*,
where they had pictures of lizards
larger than me (imagine!)
and finches with all different kinds of beaks,
depending on which island they lived on
and what they had to eat.

I got a short letter back:

My dearest Tillie:

I am quite well and, as always, love hearing from you.

I am preparing for a quick trip to Boston with a few of my teacher friends, so this letter will be brief.

Please look for a package to arrive soon: some nourishment for the body and for the mind, too.

Your loving sister,
Lila

WILLY AMOS

Ever since our blast furnace shut down
and Pa got laid off, he's been tryin'
to make his livin' as a handyman.
But it's tough—
'specially when you're colored
and the folks you're workin' for are white
and don't pay you near enough.

We hear places up north are doin' better,
but here in Dayton, stores are closed,
owners have moved away. Pa says:
"Some days, Will, I do wonder why we stay."

Then I say: "Where would we go? We got no
motorcar, no family to speak of,
'ceptin' Uncle John in Georgia—
and he's poor as us!"

Now along comes this big fuss
'bout *ev-oh-LOO-shun* . . . Pete Sykes told me
'bout it when he was up the mountain
pickin' up rocks (what can a white boy *do*
with so many rocks?)
and I was pickin' berries to sell
on the corner of Maple and Pine,
a penny for two pints.

Yep, he told me 'bout it . . . But, shoot.
I ain't understandin' it much.
Coloreds ain't allowed to go to school
with whites, and since there ain't no school
for us anywhere near here,
it's all just monkey business to me.

But I do understand some things *real* good . . .
Like me and Pa workin' ourselves half to death,
us bein' dog-tired for almost no pay,
even goin' hungry some days.

At least we run our own lives—
and that suits me and Pa just fine.
Long as we don't make no trouble
(and we don't), we come and go as we please.

So if those five white men
who Pete said met at Robinson's
think that gettin' a bunch of fancy city lawyers
and news reporters to come here
in mid-July
for a trial 'bout the Bible
and some monkeys who turned into men . . .
if they think that will
        line our pockets,
          fill our bellies,
            and maybe give us
              a little bit of fun—

well, shoot . . . you won't
hear me complainin'!

BETTY BARKER

The devil is a wise one, oh yes!
I have seen his wickedness,
his handiwork among the young.

Dayton children were once
    obedient,
    trustworthy,
    modest . . .

but they have become
    shameless,
    rebellious,
    lustful.

The girls bare their shoulders and knees.
They smoke and dance at speakeasies.
They read magazines full of filth.
They neck in the backseats of Model T's.

The boys are addicted to jazz.
They buy dancing shoes instead of work boots.
They cruise through town in their cars.
Bootleg whiskey and Hollywood flicks
make them lazier than ticks.

It was just a matter of time
till the devil sent us

a teacher like J. T. Scopes
to lead them further astray.

But I have struggled with the devil before . . .
I know his plan. He will first turn the young
from the church—the rest will follow,
swallowing the hollow promise
of "individual freedom" and "progress."

Betty Barker is a wise one, oh yes!
She is ready. She is armed for battle.
She must save these children
from their wicked, wicked ways.

JIMMY LEE DAVIS

Cross my heart
& hope to swallow
a fishhook. This is
the gospel truth:

Pete & me, we were
both in biology class
the day our regular teacher

was home, sick in bed,
& Mr. Scopes came in
to teach instead.
He assigned us the chapter
in our textbook
on evolution, & he reviewed
some of the main ideas . . .
like how the earth
was once too hot
for any life—so hot
you could fry an egg
almost anywhere on
the ground. But then it
cooled & there were some
teeny-tiny single-celled animals—
"smaller even than our
Tennessee no-see-ums," he said;
& then later, sea creatures
(that was the best part,
I thought—when all
the fish showed up),
& then slowly over years
& years, some of *them*
grew legs (a little like the
tadpoles in Connor's Pond,
I reckon) & they came
up on land & changed,
over millions *more* years,
into reptiles & mammals.

Land sakes! Mr. Scopes said
that man was a mammal,
but he never actually said
that humans were once
creatures that looked
a lot like apes
& lived in caves. (Pete saw
a picture of this in
a library book in Memphis.
He said Charles Darwin
thinks this is how
people used to look.)
Mr. Scopes never
actually taught us
anything like *that*.

When our regular teacher
came back, he asked
if we'd read that chapter
& we said yes,
& he said good,
& we moved on.

Cross my heart
& hope to swallow
a dragonfly.
That's the gospel truth.

CONSTABLE FRAYBEL

Got a call from the sheriff over
in Morgan Springs—said he had Betty Barker
in custody, and could I
"please come (soon!) to get her"?

I did not believe him.

The sheriff pointed the receiver
toward the door of the cell
so I could hear Betty tell
the rest of the inmates they were all
sinners who were going
straight to hell.

"Yep, that's her," I said. "Be right over."

I found out later how Betty had gone
down to the dance hall,
stood by the door, and handed out slips
of paper with Bible verses
as the young people went in
(nothing illegal about that). But when

she recognized a girl from her church,
Betty grabbed her, tried to cover her
bare shoulders with a sweater, tried to wipe
the color off her lips.

The girl attempted to defend herself,
hit Betty with her purse,
and pretty soon both of them
were scratching and screaming and bleeding.

Aside from bootlegging,
there's so little crime in Rhea County,
almost anybody taken into custody
makes the headlines.

As I drove the ten miles to Morgan Springs,
I couldn't help picturing
Betty Barker's name in next week's paper
under "Criminal Incidents and Arrests,"
and I predict
Betty's Bible study ladies
might be taking the next week off
to reflect.

PART 2

Does any scientist tell you where life began?
Science wants to commence with an evolution
that begins with nothing and ends nowhere.

—William Jennings Bryan, prosecution lawyer,
as quoted in the *Des Moines Register*,
July 17, 1925

The truth is no coward. It does not need
the protection of the law or the forces of
government. It does not need the protection
of even Mr. Bryan.

—Dudley Malone, defense lawyer,
as quoted in the *Des Moines Register*,
July 17, 1925

TILLIE STACKHOUSE

"Monkey Trial to Start This Week in Dayton!"
screamed this morning's headline
in the *Chattanooga Times*.
Monkey Trial? Makes it sound more like
a circus
than a court case.

After I read my *Times*, I walked to the post office,
where Eddie Spitzer brought me a brown box
that smelled of butter and sugar.
"Guess your sister has baked you another batch.
Might you be bringing some to church?"
I assured him I would.

The postmark said July 3, only four days ago,
and it was marked URGENT.
When I lifted that box, I knew
something else was in it, too.
But I didn't want anyone *else* to know.

Back outside, I took my time, walked slow,
stopped to talk with Fred Robinson,
who was taping paper monkey faces
to his front window (maybe *he* should run for Senate),
and to our school superintendent, Walter White,
who was handing out a flyer entitled
"Why Dayton of All Places?"
Walter is trying to persuade
the tourists and reporters arriving for the trial
that Dayton is the perfect place
to live and work.
(Walter should definitely run for Senate!)

At the Mansion, I took that package
to the kitchen, ripped off the string,
and plunged my fist into three layers
of my sister's homemade sugar cookies. My stomach
grumbled as I fished around the bottom—

and sure enough, wrapped in the headlines
of the *New York Times*, I found
a thick book with a green cover
that smelled of cookie dough and newsprint
all mixed together. I turned it over:
On the Origin of Species by Means of Natural Selection
by Charles Darwin.

I sat down that very minute
and started to read.

JIMMY LEE DAVIS

Tar & feather me
if this ain't so:
Mr. Robinson says
his profits are up
1,000 percent!
It's only fair, I guess,
since it was partly
his idea
to arrest Mr. Scopes
& get the ACLU
to send their best
defense lawyers here.

The newspapers have told
the whole world
that some famous lawyer
(Clarence Darrow's his name)
will defend Mr. Scopes,
& the best preacher in
the entire United States,
William Jennings Bryan
(Mama has a framed
picture of him when he
was running for president
on her dresser),
will speak against evolution

& in favor of
the Bible's version
of man's creation.
Starting yesterday,
folks from far away
came flooding into town,
like trout into a cool,
clear river. Whole families
are renting bedrooms,
pitching tents, sleeping
in cars or on benches.

Meanwhile,
Mr. Robinson's hired
Pete & me
to stock his drugstore
shelves. But we're not
stocking them with aspirin
& stomach seltzers, or with
bandages, smelling salts,
& linseed oil. No, sir . . .
We are filling as many
shelves as we can
with *monkeys*.
So far, we've unloaded:
    6 boxes of stuffed monkeys,
    3 boxes of carved monkeys,
    4 boxes of paper monkeys,
which most of the
other store owners

have bought from us
to tape up
in their own
front windows.
We even sold one
to Constable Fraybel,
who put it on his motorcycle,
with a little sign I made:
MONKEYTOWN POLICE.

Whoooeeeee!
This Monkey Trial
is gonna be *fun*.

PETER SYKES

While Mr. Robinson was busy serving up
his "Simian Sodas" at the fountain
and bragging about Dayton to some reporters,

Jimmy and me each put a stuffed monkey
on our shoulders and danced around in the back.
We scratched under our armpits, dragged our knuckles

on the floor, and had a fake fight over an apple
from my lunch. Puckering up our lips,
we were making *ooooo oooo ooooo* sounds

like we were apes, when up the back alley
rolls this delivery truck with New York plates.
We tied on our aprons, thinking it was another

load of souvenirs. But before we even had
a chance to roll up our sleeves and clear
a space on the floor, the boss comes hurrying back,

waving us toward the door. "Relax, boys. I'll get
this one myself. . . ." The driver unlocked the back
of the truck, helped Mr. Robinson climb in.

It was dark. All's we could see was a crate
made of wood and chicken wire, covered with a tarp.
All's we could hear was some scratching

and Mr. Robinson whispering something.
When the boss came out, he was leading a real
live monkey, about three feet tall, dressed

in a little tweed suit, bow tie, and straw hat.
That tiny ape-man waddled along, holding on to
the boss's hand like he was a long-lost cousin

who'd just come for a visit. "Boys,"
said Mr. Robinson, proud as a new father,
"say hello to Joe Mendi."

ERNEST MCMANUS

Ever since I was small, I've felt the calling.
Sundays, in the pews between their parents,
the other boys tugged at their suits,
tied knots in their laces,
counted the minutes.

Not me.

I sat with rapt attention, taking in every word
our pastor said. I couldn't get enough of Sunday school—
the apostles and the prophets,
the healings and miracles of Jesus. I felt as much
at home in the church
as in my mother's kitchen.

I've been a Methodist minister
for more than thirty years,
and human nature still amazes me.
I may never understand why some folks
push our Lord into a little box,
by insisting, "You must say this—you must do this—
you must *think* this."

If my years have taught me anything, it's
this: there are many roads to God
and all men and women
have a right to choose their own.

And yet . . . there are those who want to set
a tollbooth at every junction, demanding
that you pay and pay and pay,
that you walk *only* on the road they have walked,
the only one *they* say is open.

I've traveled a bit. Seen almost every part
of our great country, but not
Tennessee. So—I'm taking my entire
two weeks' vacation
in Dayton. I want to hear W. J. Bryan,
that great orator,
and Clarence Darrow, the most clever
and brilliant lawyer of our time,
argue the origins of the human race.

And when it's all over, I hope we're not
afraid to embrace
our God-given minds.

MARYBETH DODD

Daddy's cousin Tillie Stackhouse
manages the Mansion, a boardinghouse
where several defense lawyers

and some reporters
are staying. Tillie's a hard worker,
but she likes to taste her cooking
as much as serve it.

So when she came hurrying up the street this morning,
all panicked and the sweat rolling off her brow,
I thought she might faint
right in our yard.
I made her sit down quick,
pumped her a cup of cold water.

"Marybeth . . . I'm just not used to this,"
she said after she'd caught her breath.
"Every room's full up and I can't get
food to the tables fast enough.
Could you come help . . . just till the trial's done?"

I knew Daddy wouldn't like me working
anywhere but home. He's never said so
in front of Tillie, but he's dead set against women
running any kind of business. Since Mama died,
he doesn't let me handle money
except what he gives me
to buy our clothing and food.

But see here—I'm almost seventeen!
I do believe it's time I had my own job,
my own money to spend as I please.
Besides . . . wouldn't helping one of Daddy's kin

be the Christian thing to do?
I decided it would.
If Daddy gave me trouble about it, I'd tell him,
"It's only temporary."

Tillie waited patiently while I
argued all this in my head.

"What time you need me?" I finally said.

She grinned, patted my cheek.
"Quarter past four. Marybeth, you're
a good girl. If your daddy gives you any lip,
tell him to come see Tillie!"

I watched her amble away,
her big strong frame taking up the whole sidewalk.
Daddy, I was pretty sure,
would not be giving me
much lip.

ERNEST McMANUS

A convention of that religious order
the Holy Rollers
has come together in the nearby hills.

After dinner, when the town quiets down,
you can hear them
over the finger-tapping reporters
and the clanking dishes
and the dogs scavenging leftovers.

If you listen, you can hear them
howling and screaming
as they roll on the ground in a frenzy,
a state they claim
comes to those among them who are touched
by the Holy Spirit.

Until yesterday, I could not say
I'd had the pleasure
of such an experience.

But then, it wasn't until yesterday
that I took a walk in the Mansion garden,
stopping to relish the smell
of a patch of yellow daisies
where bees buzzed by the dozens
and one found its way into my trousers.

I must've looked a sight,
hopping and yelling and shaking my leg
trying to expel the misguided bug.
By the time I shook him out,
there was a small crowd assembled on the porch
and four Holy Rollers,
who'd come into town that afternoon,
came over to congratulate me
on being saved.

TILLIE STACKHOUSE

Too often this season, I've seen Willy Amos
at the corner of Market and Pine,
selling little green pears or pints of wild berries,
two for a penny. Since the furnace closed down,
the Amoses have had it worse
than most in this town.
David Amos is the best handyman around,
but most folks pay him less
than a white worker.

But Lord willing, while this trial's in Dayton,
maybe I can offer a way

to make things a little more even.
I was thinking on how, exactly, I might do that

when I saw Betty Barker brush right past Willy
on her way to a prayer meeting.
Willy offered her a pear, but Betty just
ignored him—clutched her Good Book
tighter to her chest and hurried past
without even a kind look.

Not far behind came Minnie Bly,
the "crazy mountain lady." Poor as dirt,
Minnie lives in the hills on what she gathers or shoots,
never goes to church, comes to town just
to trade pelts for supplies.

Minnie stopped, talked to Willy for a while.
Then she walked across to the grocery,
where I was inside, buying cornstarch
to make a bee sting poultice
for one of my boarders.

Minnie traded two fine coonskins
for three loaves of bread, some cheese,
and four jars of jam. Minnie took one loaf
and one jar for herself, put the rest in a sack,
and gave it to Willy, who tried to give it back,
but Minnie waved him off.

Up the street, Betty Barker and her Bible study ladies
were hanging a banner
on the courthouse. READ YOUR BIBLE! it said.

When Minnie Bly walked by, Betty cried:
"If there be any wicked way in me . . .
lead me in the way everlasting!—Psalm one thirty-nine!"

Minnie Bly just smiled.

WILLY AMOS

Three dollars, seventy-five cents!

I counted it ten times.
I folded and unfolded the bills,
ran the coins in my pocket
through my fingers,
and my, my . . . they do feel mighty fine!

Here's how I come by
so much dough . . .

Miz Stackhouse,
one of the best white folks in Dayton,
she come runnin' up to me
pantin' and sweatin' in the July heat.

"Willy Amos!" she shouts.
"You be at the train station at three o'clock.
You meet those reporters and lawyers
coming in from the city
and you say you'll help them carry their cases
and find places to stay. . . ."

Miz Stackhouse, she's a big, big lady.
She was breathin' hard as a racehorse
in that street-corner sun.
I took her arm, moved us under a big old maple
so's she feels cooler.

She pats my cheek. "You're a good man, Willy,"
she says. "I'll pay you a quarter
for every lawyer or reporter
you bring to the Mansion. Then those men
should be tipping you
for taking their suitcases from the train,
and if they don't . . . you come get me, hear?"

I did as Miz Stackhouse said.
I went to the train station.
I helped three lawyers and five reporters

carry their cases to the Mansion
and every one of them, sure enough,
gives me a tip.

I ain't believin' things can get
much better. Then Miz Stackhouse,
she gives me the tallest glass of lemonade
I ever seen, and while I drink it,
she hands me a writin' slate and a box of chalk.
"My sister, Lila, just sent me a new one
for my kitchen lists," she says.
"I'm looking for someone to take this 'un
off my hands . . . you reckon you know
someone like that?"

"Yes, ma'am," I say while I think on how
many words and numbers I might write
before this chalk runs out.
"Yes, ma'am . . . I reckon I do."

MARYBETH DODD

The American Civil Liberties Union has sent
Clarence Darrow

to defend Mr. Scopes
against the State of Tennessee
for teaching evolution at Rhea County High.

Daddy told me:
Clarence Darrow
recently defended two teenage boys
who confessed to killing another boy
just for a thrill,
and even though they were clearly guilty,
he convinced the jury
not to sentence them to death.

Tillie told me:
Clarence Darrow
defended folks who were too poor or too hated
against those who were too rich (or too celebrated),
and that he also defended
colored people and mistreated workers
because he believes everyone is equal
under the law.

The papers said:
Clarence Darrow
is coming to Dayton by train and private car,
all the way from Chicago—
where they have jazz clubs and baseball and gangsters—
and a small news reception
will be held for him at the train station.

I didn't think Daddy would let me go,
but when I mentioned
(real casual as I was kneading wheat bread dough)
that I might walk down there
to sneak a peek, Daddy said:
"I'm too tired, but you go on ahead."

The way most townfolks have been talking,
I thought Clarence Darrow
would look like the devil himself, complete
with a tail and horns and a pitchfork.
Well.
Clarence Darrow does not look like
the devil himself.
He looks more like a well-weathered farmer
or like someone's eccentric grandfather.

I got a real good look as he passed by.
His eyes (gray-blue, lively but kind)
were set deep in his wrinkled face
and he wore a suit that didn't fit right.
His suspenders were red and blue, colors I might
make an apron or a tablecloth with.
His gait was slow and easy,
like he didn't want to be noticed,
like he didn't mind mixing in
with the rest of us.

Pete Sykes was there, too.
Like me, he wanted to see

what the most famous lawyer in America
looked like.

"Seems pretty regular, don't he?"
I had to agree.

"Stop by Robinson's sometime, Marybeth,"
Pete said before he left.

"I'll fix you a Simian Soda for free."
(That was real sweet.)

When I told Daddy I'd seen Clarence Darrow,
he said: "That low-down no-'count lawyer . . .
got no right coming here,
telling us what to believe.
If you have any sense, Marybeth,
you won't pay him no mind!"

And later, when I told Tillie
what Daddy thought, she said:
"Your father's entitled to his opinion.
But you're a smart girl, Marybeth—
trust your instincts. God made those, too!"

I admit, from the moment I laid eyes on
Clarence Darrow,
there was something about him
I just plain liked.
He has a quiet kind of energy—
like a big old dog that's happy
to eat and nap on the porch . . .

but everyone knows not to
disturb him
while he's lying there guarding your door.

PAUL LEBRUN

Quarter past five. That's when I arrived
at the Dayton train station.
It was exactly forty-eight hours since I'd left
the *St. Louis Post-Dispatch* newsroom,
my editor yelling after me: "Lebrun!—
don't you dare come back without a story!
You wire me three thousand words a day, OK?
And don't bust that camera!"

Bone tired, my stomach knotted with hunger,
I started down the main street
looking for a place to spend the night.

"Hey, kid!" I said to a red-haired lad
with fishing lures hanging from his belt.
"Where might I find a warm meal
and a place to sleep?"
He finished hanging a sign that said

IT ALL STARTED HERE!
above the drugstore door.

"Over to the Mansion's where everybody's going,"
he said, pointing down the street. "Hey, mister!
We got stuffed monkeys, two for a dollar.
You interested?"

A businessman in the making, I thought.
"I'll sleep on your offer," I told him.

Now I confess—
I had pegged these fundamentalists
as folks with no imaginations,
but when I saw the lopsided clapboard house
behind the sign that said THE MANSION,
I knew I was wrong.

A heavyset lady gave me a towel, clean sheets,
and the best meat loaf dinner
I've ever eaten.

"Son, you look plumb tuckered out," she said,
patting me on the cheek. "Room's upstairs—
second on the right. You go on up now,
have a good night!"

I lay down on the cot
in my freshly painted room.
I drifted off counting the words

two thousand ninety-eight, two thousand ninety-nine . . .
I needed to wire
so I wouldn't be fired.

JIMMY LEE DAVIS

Confused as a firefly
in a jelly jar—
that's how I feel.

Before Pete
went to see
Clarence Darrow
at the train station,
he asked me if
I wanted to come
along. I don't know
much about
Mr. Darrow,
& I don't have
much to say
about evolution
(except about the
sea creatures part,

which I kinda like . . .).
But I *do* know
if I went to the
station to see
Clarence Darrow,
it would upset Mama
something awful.
Ever since my
older brother Bobby
left the church,
left town,
fell in with the
wrong crowd,
& spent two years
behind bars (nearly
did Mama in, it did)—
I am real careful
not to disappoint her.

About this trial
Mama says:
"Jimmy Lee—you
are a baptized
Methodist Christian
& I will not
let you stray
like your brother did;
there's hell to pay
when you wander!

Jimmy Lee—it's
your duty, while
this Monkey Trial's
in town, to stand up
for the Bible
as the true, the
only, word of God."

The way I see it,
that means
taking the side of
the prosecution, the side
against Mr. Scopes,
the side that cheers
for W. J. Bryan,
Bible champion.
So I told Pete,
"I don't want
to see Mr. Darrow
at the train station,
'cause he believes
in things that are
against my religion."
Pete just stood
in the street,
shaking his head.
"Jimmy Lee, you
& me, we've been
best friends

since first grade.
I don't want this
Monkey Trial
to be a thing
that comes
between us."

Lord's truth—
neither do I.

PART 3

When science strikes upon that which man's eternal hope is founded, then I say the foundation of man's civilization is about to crumble.

—Thomas Stewart, attorney general for the State of Tennessee

We have just had a war with twenty million dead. Civilization is not so proud of the work of adults. . . . For God's sake let the children have their minds kept open—close no doors to their knowledge. Shut no door from them. Make the distinction between theology and science. Let them have both. Let them both be taught. Let them both live.

—Dudley Malone, defense lawyer

WILLY AMOS

Ever since Dayton's gone wild
for the Monkey Trial,
me and Pa have barely slept.
The town council's plannin' a big dinner
for W. J. Bryan, so we got hired
to string up lights and slap together
twenty tables in the church basement.

Then we put in ten
new toilets (I got to try one, too—
pretty nice!) over to the courthouse
and gave the main room
a fresh coat of paint.

Just when I'm thinkin' we're through,
the supervisor tells us the jury box—
sittin' smack in the middle—
would block the view for the movie crews. . . .
So me, Pete, and Jimmy Lee, we

moved the whole thing off to the side
so's Pa could build a platform for the cameras
right in front of the judge.
(Pa got worried that movin' the jury
would make the judge angry,
but the supervisor says, "Judge is all for it!")

Next, Constable Fraybel took us
to the Millman farm,
where me, Pete, and Jimmy Lee, we
painted thick white lines down both sides
of the upper pasture for a runway.

"Imagine, boys," the constable said
as he drove us back to town. "In a week or so,
planes will come and go
from this here airfield
with films of our Monkey Trial
to show at movie theaters all across the USA!"

By then, Jimmy Lee was near asleep,
Pete was brushin' off some rocks he'd found
in the field, and I was too tuckered out
to do any imaginin'.

Back in town, we saw even more folks
sellin' food, Bibles, and books
all the way up Market Street. Seems like this
Monkey Trial's gettin' to be
a big deal.

Well, I ain't never met a judge before, never seen
a real trial. But, shoot—you can bet
with all the work we've done already,
I'll be seein' *plenty* of this one.

CONSTABLE FRAYBEL

You would think the Tennessee state fair
had come to Market Street.

Every enterprising person
from here to Morgan Springs
has slapped up a stand or a table
where you can buy:

sandwiches,
ice cream,
soda pop,
hot dogs,
cinnamon squares,
blueberry pie.

Eddie at the post office told me
the souvenir vendors

placed a rush order today
for more ape masks and buttons that say:
YOUR OLD MAN'S A MONKEY!

The famous preacher T. T. Martin
arrived with his truckload of books,
and by the way it looks,
his latest title: *Hell and the High School*
is a real hot sell.
(I was surprised to see Jimmy Lee
helping T. T. Martin . . . though you can't
fault the boy for his hard working.)

So far, though, everyone's been
orderly and polite; so far there hasn't been
a single fight
over who sells what and where,
for how long or how much.

I read the papers, same as anybody. They say
times are good in places like
Detroit, New York, Chicago,
where they have factories and assembly lines,
fancy restaurants, and music shows.
But here in east Tennessee, where farming
and family business are still the way,
rich folks are scarce as hen's teeth.

I've had a few complaints from the
newspaper people

'cause they can't drive down Market Street
(I've closed most of it to automobiles),
but as Dayton's only constable,
I thought it my duty
to allow any decent, hardworking citizen
of Rhea County
with a table and something to sell
to set up along the sidewalk
and make himself
an extra buck.

ERNEST McMANUS

I have followed
the political, legal, and liturgical careers
of William Jennings Bryan
for the last thirty years.

Mr. Bryan is, without a doubt,
one of the finest orators in America,
a celebrated minister,
and a three-time candidate for president.

Clarence Darrow, in fact, campaigned
on Bryan's behalf, and rumor has it

that despite their philosophic differences,
they have kept a close friendship.

This evening, W. J. Bryan gave a speech
in the little park near the courthouse,
a speech that drew people in
like bees to a bottle of syrup.

He talked for almost an hour
on the virtues of majority rule, on the power
of the taxpayer's checkbook in the schools,
on the evils of modern science.

I had it in my mind
to raise my hand and
ask him what he thought about:

modern transportation (like the steam train he rode here
    or the nice car he owns at his Florida home)

medicine (like the aspirin his wife takes for her arthritis)

mass communication (he announced, with great pride,
    that our Monkey Trial will be broadcast live by WGN)

Trains, aspirin, microphones, radios . . .
unless I've misread my Bible, none of those
was around in Adam's time,
and every one was a scientific invention.

But I didn't raise my hand.
I didn't have the heart—the man
was so clearly enjoying
the sound of his own voice,
it would have been
a sin
to interrupt him.

TILLIE STACKHOUSE

"How do you know for sure
if someone's a Christian?"

That's what Marybeth asked me this morning
while we were pegging up sheets on the line.

"Well," I said, "that depends on who you ask. . . .
Betty Barker would say
you must attend every Bible study and
every prayer meeting, you must never
wear makeup, and you must dress respectfully.
You must never seek more knowledge
than what the Bible provides."

(Cookbooks and sewing manuals are fine,
but read nothing
that contradicts your minister.)

"Well, I won't ever be a Christian
by that definition!" Marybeth laughed.

"Now, if you ask Fred Robinson and Walter White,"
I continued, "they'd say be a good citizen.
Support Dayton and its businesses. Work hard
and help your neighbor. Don't drink . . .
but visit the soda fountain often.
Rest on the Sabbath. Celebrate Christmas.
Vote in every election."

"And what if you asked Minnie Bly?" she asked.

I could tell she'd been thinkin' on this one.
She doesn't miss much, that Marybeth.

"Minnie Bly, she'd most likely say
there's no such thing as a Christian. She'd tell you
Christianity is just a conspiracy
by men in robes
to get you to obey, to get more money in the offering,
to get you to sit before them every Sunday
and feel ashamed for being human."

It was quiet while we pegged up more sheets.

"What if I asked *you?*" Marybeth finally said.

I couldn't help thinking
how much she was like my sister.
When we were younger, Lila was always reading
and wondering and pestering me with questions.
I kinda liked it, though.
"You know that small wooden sign
above my sofa?" I asked.
"The one that says
DO UNTO OTHERS AS YOU WOULD
HAVE THEM DO UNTO YOU?"
Marybeth nodded.

"Well, it's been handed
down through my family for years. . . .
My great-great-grandfather carved it.
He never set foot in a church, but everyone
loved him. And though he was poor,
he never turned away a stranger
who needed a meal or a place to sleep, never
turned his back on the unlucky or the sick."

Lila had told me that teaching's mostly about
giving good examples.
So I rummaged around in my brain
for one to give Marybeth.

"Once," I said, "he walked four miles carrying
a newborn colt whose mother
had strayed off and died. Stayed up all night
with the farmer who owned it, keeping it alive.
That colt grew up to be a prize-winning sire
and earned that farmer enough to retire.

"Now that I'm older," I told her,
"I aim to keep things simple. But I do believe
if Jesus walked into my parlor
and we shared some tea and apple pie,
he'd agree that my granddaddy's sign
captures his message just fine. . . .
And I expect, Marybeth, to live a few years yet;
but when I die,
I'm leaving that sign to you."

When all the sheets were hung,
we stood on the back stoop
to admire our work.
"Looks like we're cleaning for the Klan!"
Marybeth said.

Lordy, that girl does make me laugh.

PAUL LEBRUN

I've been gathering notes
on J. T. Scopes,
who's accused of teaching evolution
to his students.

A Chicago reporter told me:
"Scopes is not a Dayton native. He came
from the same town (Salem, Illinois)
as W. J. Bryan, the man who's pledged
to do all he can to convict him."

A secretary at the high school told me:
"Mr. Scopes graduated with a science degree
from the University of Kentucky
and was hired to teach physics,
general science, and math
by the Rhea County Board of Education,
which includes a few of the men
who then had him arrested."

The young man who helped me find lodging
the night I arrived in Dayton told me:
"Mr. Scopes likes to swim, play tennis, hike,
& he's a darn fine fisherman, too!
He helps coach the football team
& fills in for the other teachers
when they're out sick."

(Scopes was, in fact, substituting
for the regular biology teacher
when he assigned the lesson on evolution.)

A young lady working at the Mansion told me:
  "Mr. Scopes goes to church, but I think
    it's mostly to meet women. . . . See, we don't
      have any jazz clubs or dance halls in Dayton,
        so where else can he get dates?"

Good point.

The more I read my notes,
the more I feel
a kinship with J. T. Scopes.
As a fledgling reporter, far from my Missouri home,
I hope I do right by this brave man
who has agreed to take a stand
against ignorance.

Like an amateur fighter, Scopes has been
bullied by his corner men
into a too-big arena
so they can make a fast dollar.
Now the poor teacher
has the whole country watching
as he holds up his gloves
and tries to fend off
a fatal blow.

JIMMY LEE DAVIS

Rich as Rockefeller,
that's how I feel.
Between my job
at Robinson's
& helping out
the foreman
at the courthouse
& sellin' books
for T. T. Martin
& painting lines
for the new airstrip
on Millman's pasture,
I have more cash
in my pocket
than a minister after
Sunday collection.
If things were
normal, me & Pete,
we'd head over
to Morgan Springs,
buy new lures & reels,
head up to Connor's Pond.
But ever since this
trial's arrived, things
aren't the same
between us. Take today,
for example: while

we were making
white lines down
both sides of the field,
Pete found a rock
with a leaf print on it.
"Bet Mr. Darwin
would know how
old this is," Pete said.
Now I know I was
in that class when
Mr. Scopes told us
to read the chapter
on evolution
& I know I didn't
think much about it
at the time. . . .
But now things
are different.
Now there's a trial
& two sides
& like Mama says:
"In this life,
you got to walk
on one side of the road
or the other . . .
and Jimmy Lee—
you know which side
the Lord wants *you* on!"
So for Mama's sake,

it looks like
I will need to stay
on her side of the street,
the side of
W. J. Bryan
& the Bible story
of creation. I told Pete:
"Only God knows
the age of that
rock & that leaf
'cause He made 'em
both on day three!"
Pete just put
that rock in his
pocket & we
didn't talk
the whole way
back to town.

PETER SYKES

When I learned to play football, I didn't
give up baseball. When I learned that

Santa Claus wasn't the one who brought
gifts, I didn't give up Christmas.

When I learned to run, I didn't give up
walking. Now that I'm learning science,

why does Jimmy Lee believe
I have given up on God?

PAUL LEBRUN

I rose before dawn after
a restless night.
I dressed quickly and went downstairs,
where the smell of meat loaf lingered, mingled
with cigar smoke and coffee.

I stepped out onto
the front porch of the Mansion
and watched the first pale rays
of pink and gold spill silently
over the hills of eastern Tennessee.

I heard the screen door behind me
open, and out stepped Professor Neal,

who had come down from Knoxville
to help Darrow defend J. T. Scopes.

We exchanged pleasantries, then turned
to watch the sun rise higher
as the sparrows, finches, and wrens
delivered a morning chorus
from the hedges.

"You know, it wasn't so long ago," Neal observed,
"that Copernicus was imprisoned for proving
the earth revolved around the sun
and not vice versa."

"And not so long before that, people believed
a man drove a golden chariot
across the sky each day, from one end
to the other," I added.

He nodded. "I always liked that story. . . ."

We were both quiet for a while.

"You think you can win here, Mr. Neal?" I asked,
rather boldly.

He shrugged. "What happens here
will mean everything—and nothing. The human mind
is such a mystery, but the law
doesn't love a mystery . . . it loves precedents

and evidence and certainty. So we'll do
our best and leave the rest
to the jury."

He smiled and went inside.

I remained on the top step,
feeling like that man in the chariot,
beginning his long, curious trip.

BETTY BARKER

I called a special meeting
of the ladies' Bible study
so that we could offer up
a prayer
for the destruction of Darwinism
and the victory
of Genesis
on this, the first day of the Monkey Trial.

Afterwards, we made a big
fire in the ditch behind the church
and we threw in
twelve copies

of Hunter's *Civic Biology*
and we all stood there
and sang "Hallelujah!"
as Darwin went up in smoke.

WILLY AMOS

It's gonna be hot. Real hot.

Millman's cows have already
gone down to the stream for the day
and our two mules
are sweatin' like they've been pullin'
a full load of hay
instead of just takin' me and Pa
into town.

We stopped at Robinson's store
for two boxes of
palm-leaf fans
that he says we can sell
at the courthouse today
and keep half the pay.

Pete Sykes and Jimmy Lee,
they're still workin' for Mr. Robinson,
but they ain't been talkin'
to each other
since they had that fight
out at Millman's place
over a rock and day three.

PAUL LEBRUN

I arrived at six forty-five—
more than two hours early.
I was sure there'd be nobody there
and I could get myself the best chair
in the courtroom.

Ha! If my editor were here, he'd say,
"Lebrun! You're young and you're smart,
but don't forget you're still an idiot."
And this time he'd be right.

I counted thirty-four photographers
out front, and lined up on the inside steps
were at least two dozen more—

plus townspeople, farmers, and Bible-toting
mountain folk, all bent on watching the trial.

A young Negro stood near the door
selling palm-leaf fans for a nickel.
It already felt like the kind of day
I'd rather spend hip-deep in a cool running stream,
so I pressed my coin into his hand,
took a sturdy fan, and hurried in.

Almost every chair at the reporters' tables
was taken. I settled myself into
the one empty seat,
took out my pen and paper,
and waited.

At eight forty-five, Judge Raulston walked solemnly
down the center of the room and told
his wife and children to sit in the first row.
As he chatted with the men from WGN,
I saw he held
a law book in one hand,
a Bible in the other.

"Wonder why he bothered to bring that,"
the reporter next to me murmured.

"The Bible?" I inquired.

"No . . . I meant the law book."

My gray-haired neighbor (his press badge
said *New York Times*) glared at me.
"Didn't you do your homework, son? This judge
is an *elected* official and a part-time
Methodist minister. This is no trial,
it's a fundamentalist revival!"

My left hand worked the palm-leaf fan
while my right hand
quoted him exactly.

TILLIE STACKHOUSE

Cleaning, I came upon a small
black notebook
stamped with the initials *J.N.*
I knew it must belong to Mr. Neal
of the defense team, and that he must have
dropped it when he got up
from his meal.

I hightailed it down Market Street,
thinking he might need it in court.

When I got there, I could hardly believe
all the people: reporters and cameramen
crowded onto the lawn, and more folks coming in
by the minute off the back roads,
riding horse-drawn wagons and dressed
in overalls and straw hats,
eager to be at ringside
when Bryan and Darrow begin
what the papers are calling
"a duel to the death."

I had made up my mind ahead of time
that I would not be squeezing myself into
that hotbox of a room
until I was darn certain
that this trial was worth all the fuss
everyone was making. But there I was,
despite my best intentions, Mr. Neal's notebook
tucked under my arm, trying to push past
the media men on the lawn and into
the front lobby, and up the stairs
to the second-floor chamber.

Now, I am not a small woman—
there's just no getting around that—
and for most of my life that's been
more of a curse than a blessing.
But today as I pushed my way inside,
my size was far from a burden.

I reached Mr. Neal, tapped his shoulder,
placed the notebook in his hand.
Lord's truth . . . his face lit up like a
Christmas candle!
He threw his skinny arms around me
and hugged me,
then pecked me on the cheek
right in front of everyone.

I know I must've looked a sight—all flushed
and perspired. I tried to politely say no
to the seat he gave me (first row!)
but Mr. Neal is a lawyer
and let me tell you,
they are *not* easily persuaded.

So that's how I got to sit
smack in the middle of the first day's events
as they read the charges against
Mr. Scopes, introduced the lawyers,
and chose the jury members
(all men, of course, most of 'em churchgoing
farmers, only one of 'em illiterate).
I forgot all about making the next meal
until the judge banged his gavel.
"This court will reconvene at nine A.M. on Monday!"

I nearly fainted when he said that.
I realized then that about thirty hungry, thirsty men

were heading to the Mansion
and when they arrived, there'd be absolutely
nothing prepared.

MARYBETH DODD

When I showed up at the Mansion
for the evening shift,
I did not find Tillie
in the kitchen preparing dinner,
or in the garden picking flowers for the tables,
or pinning up linens to dry in the yard.
I thought something bad had happened, so I

phoned Constable Fraybel.
"I saw Tillie a while back heading up to
the courthouse," he assured me.
"Prob'ly stayed at the trial awhile, Marybeth.
She'll be home soon, I expect."

I hoped he was right.

Still, it wouldn't be soon enough. . . .
I had no idea what she'd planned to feed

all the men who'd be showing up
hungry
in about half an hour.

I searched through the pantry. I sliced
and fried as many potatoes as I could find,
threw in some sausage, peppers, and onions.
By the time Tillie came panting and heaving
into the kitchen, I was standing over
three pans of the stuff.

"Thank goodness!" Tillie said, patting my cheek
and tying on her apron to help.

Turns out I'd made enough
for everyone to have a good-sized meal,
and for Mr. Darrow's dinner guest, W. J. Bryan,
to have thirds.

Pete came by after dinner
with a delivery for Tillie from Robinson's store.
He stayed around awhile
and helped me finish up washin' dishes.
(That was real sweet.)

Pete kept watching the table where
Mr. Darrow and Mr. Bryan were sharing
laughter and cigars.

"Marybeth, how do you reckon
they stay friends," Pete asked, "if they don't even
believe the same thing?"

"Don't quite know," I answered.
"Maybe they just put that part of them
aside
when they're together? . . ."

Pete got real quiet.

"Trial's only been on for one day," I reminded him.
"Might not be so easy to put things
aside
if it lasts for a long time."

"Yep," Pete said, "I know. . . .
I hope they try, though."

PART 4

The Tennessee case has uncovered the conspiracy against . . . Christianity.

—William Jennings Bryan, prosecution lawyer

I have never tried to impose my views of religion on any human being that ever lived. I have a right to my own views and would fight as hard to protect every other man's views as I would my own.

—Clarence Darrow, defense lawyer

JIMMY LEE DAVIS

Madder than a
slapped hornet—
that's how I felt.

Me & Pete got
into a fight
over who should
take Joe Mendi
up to the second
day of the trial.
Pete said *he* should
'cause he's worked
here three days
longer than me,
so he's got
seniority.
I said I should
'cause I had
a better nose

for business.
Pete said: "No,
you just got
a bigger mouth!"
That's when we
stopped arguing
& started swinging
& Mr. Robinson
came running:
"Hey, hey!—
What's gotten
into you boys?
Next man throws
a punch loses
his job." The boss
flipped a nickel
high into the air
& I yelled, "*Tails!*"
& it *was* tails,
& so I got to go
to the courthouse
with the monkey
to stir up some
publicity
for the store.

It was fun at first—
Joe Mendi in his
little trousers,
suspenders,

& T-shirt with
SHOP AT ROBINSON'S
in bold print
across the front.
But when he saw
the blind organ
grinder's monkey,
he wiggled free
& chased that
poor little ape clear
down Market Street.

Lord! I thought
I'd catch it
from the boss
for letting such a
ruckus loose.
After some hard
running & a lot
of yelling, I finally
got Joe Mendi
back. At the store,
I made sure
to tell Mr. Robinson
how all the
photographers
at the courthouse
had taken pictures of
"the great Dayton
monkey chase."

The boss patted me
on the back.
"Well done, son!
You deserve
a raise. . . ."

Whew! I felt
luckier than a
tick on a dog's
back. I may not
have a way with
animals, but I
seem to have
a knack for
timing.

PETER SYKES

When I lost the coin toss to Jimmy Lee,
I figured I'd be stacking wooden monkeys
till noon. But when Jimmy came back early,

with Joe Mendi tied to his hand
(I guess Mr. Robinson got his publicity,

just not the way he planned),

the boss sent *me* downtown with a load
of ape masks and a box of paper fans.
I stood with the rest of the courthouse crowd

on the side lawn, hawking souvenirs, thinking
about Marybeth's golden hair and hoping
she might decide to come by and say hi.

But I didn't have a whole lot of free time
to think—in less than an hour, I was sold out.
I knew me and Jimmy Lee would just start

arguing more if I went back to the store,
so I decided to stay and watch
day two of the Monkey Trial.

I swear it must've been
one hundred degrees in that room,
packed to busting as it was

with reporters, photographers, lawyers,
and just plain Dayton townsfolk
all jostling for position up front.

I took in my wooden box,
found a spot in the back, and stood
on top. I could see pretty good

as the attorney general read
the formal charges against Mr. Scopes
while the dozen jury men sat there

grinning, in case the photographers
were taking pictures. Judge Raulston
asked Mr. Neal of the defense team

how he wished to plead, and Mr. Neal
said that he wanted the charge
against Mr. Scopes "quashed."

I had no idea what that meant,
and by all the whispering around me,
neither did anyone else. Constable Fraybel

was also in the back, so I asked:
"Hey, Constable—what's *quashed*?"
and he said, "Canceled." I was still a little

confused. "It means," he explained, "if
Mr. Scopes is accused of breaking a law
that is itself not a fair one,

then the law itself has to be
judged by a higher court, and all this
will be pretty pointless."
I thought about what he said. "You mean

the trial might be done before it gets going?"
The constable nodded. "Yep, pretty much."

I looked at Judge Raulston with his law book
off to one side, his left wrist resting
on the Holy Bible. Earlier, when I was outside

on the lawn near the loudspeakers, I'd heard
a minister giving the opening prayer—
"Dear Lord, the creator of the heaven

and the earth and the sea and all that is
in them"—and I knew then that
Mr. Neal's request to quash the charges

would get about as far
as me asking Jimmy Lee
for a loan of fifty dollars.

ERNEST McMANUS

Because the motion made by Mr. Neal
to quash the indictment did not
involve the jury, but just the judge,

and the judge did not wish to prejudice,
in any way, the twelve men who will

have to decide (*if* this trial continues)
if Mr. Scopes is innocent or guilty,
the jury was sent swiftly
out of the courtroom with the bailiff.
We all listened to the team of lawyers
defending Mr. Scopes as they argued

to have the charges against him dropped.
Arthur Hays, Dudley Malone, and John Neal
all claimed that the Butler Act—
which is the official name of the law
that forbids the teaching of evolution
in the Tennessee public schools—

was unconstitutional because it favored
the Christian religion over all others.
They also argued that Darwin's ideas
did not contradict the Bible because
thousands of devout Christians

believed in both God *and* evolution.
The Butler Act, they said, clearly
went against the state mandate
"to cherish science and literature."
Well, I thought that was plenty
to contemplate for one day, but then

it was the prosecution's turn: McKenzie,
Hicks, and Stewart all claimed
that Scopes was supposed to teach
only what he was *hired* to teach,
and that he "willfully" broke the law.

They said no preference was given
to the Christian religion,
and that people across the country
understood perfectly what the law meant—
and were all for it.

Then Clarence Darrow stood up to give
the final argument for the defense.
A hush fell over the entire room.
He spoke for several minutes,
his voice starting slow and calm,

then picking up speed like a train
rushing down a steep river valley.
"I doubt if there is a person in Tennessee,"
he proclaimed, "who does not know
that the God in which they believe did not

finish creation on the first day, but that he is still
working to make something better and higher . . .
out of human beings." After court let out,
I heard McKenzie, an opposing lawyer,
say to Darrow: "That was the greatest speech

I ever heard in my life on any subject."

A lady handing out pamphlets disagreed:

"Heathen! Godless infidel!" she declared

as Mr. Darrow settled himself in a chair

with a well-deserved glass of lemonade.

WILLY AMOS

When Clarence Darrow speaks,
everyone in the whole courtroom
listens.

I guess that's what it's like
when your teacher speaks in school,
but since there ain't no school
I can go to,
I have to take *my* learnin' where I can.

Like the year I was sick with fever . . .
Pa took me to see a doctor
in Morgan Springs, and sick as I was,
I begged him for a look

at one of the hundred books
on shelves in his office.

"They're mostly medical manuals, Will,"
Doc told me. "But there are a few on
philosophy, geography, history,
and one or two on English grammar . . .
you can come by and borrow them
anytime you like."

That was three years back.
I been readin' them books
and copyin' down the words at night
by candlelight ever since.
I can't know for sure, but I reckon
I can read and write
good as most kids in Dayton.

Still, "no one wants to hire a *thinkin' Negro*"—
least that's what Pa says.
"You best keep your learnin' deep in your
pockets 'round most white folks, you hear?"

"Miz Stackhouse, she knows I can
read and write—
it don't bother her none," I argued.

"She ain't like most white folks," Pa said.
"You best be careful. . . ."

And my Bible—now *that's* a hard book.
Sometimes I don't rightly know
what all them strange words mean:
begot, betrothed, slain, smote . . .
But somewhere in there it says:
There is a time for everything
under heaven. . . .

So I keep prayin' for a time when I won't
need to hide my learnin'
from anyone.

MARYBETH DODD

I must've fallen asleep reading.
When I woke, it was already half past
four and I was late for work.
I left dinner on the table for Daddy,
tucked my hair into a bun,
grabbed my apron,
and ran to the Mansion.

When I arrived, seven men I'd never
seen before in Dayton
were posing for a photograph on the lawn.
I went and stood on the porch steps
next to Tillie. "Experts!" she whispered.
"Darrow's brought 'em in to testify for Scopes."

We watched them swelter
in the late-day Tennessee heat,
sweat running down their faces,
staining their nice white shirts.

When the photographer finally said,
"OK—*done!*" they scrambled onto the porch,
out of the sun.
Me and Tillie took up our pitchers,
poured ice-cold lemonade for everyone.

"Gentlemen!" the photographer said.
"Before I go, I'll need to know
your full names, school locations, and occupations
for my captions."

They kept drinking and talking.
I kept pouring and listening. Turns out,
they came to Dayton from

Missouri,
  Maryland,

Illinois,
New Jersey,
Texas—

and each one taught some
scientific subject:

zoology,
geology,
anthropology,
biology

at a university.

Lordy! I don't think I was ever so close
to so much intelligence.
I wondered how long it took to get
qualified
to teach at a university.

I wondered
what that might be like.

JIMMY LEE DAVIS

Next to God
& fishing, I love
baseball best.
'Specially
the Yankees.
I never been
to New York
(heck, I been no
farther than
Morgan Springs),
but I root for
the Yanks
on account of
Lou Gehrig.
This year
their manager
put Gehrig
at first base
to replace
Wally Pipp
& so far he's
batting .428
& he's aiming
for .450 or I'm
a catfish!
It's heaven when

I'm sitting at the
soda fountain,
listening to the
crack of Gehrig's
bat, the roar
of the crowd
on the radio.
I imagine going
to the games
is a lot like
going to church:
people get
dressed up, leave
their homes,
& come together
in one big place—
they do a lot of
standing up
& sitting down
& when their
team's behind,
they do some
praying, too.
There's even
organ music!

Pete & me
used to listen
to the games

together, try to
guess which
player'd get
the next hit,
or which pitch
the pitcher
would throw.

We don't do that
now, though.
My hand's still
sore from our
fistfight.
Lou Gehrig
just hit another
home run. Why
don't I feel
like cheering?

PAUL LEBRUN

Fortified by five of Robinson's cherry Cokes,
I had my interview with J. T. Scopes.

The whole time we talked, he was not
angry or resentful or afraid.

He was just surprised at all the fuss
being made over the fact that,

as a substitute, he had reviewed a chapter
on evolution with some upperclassmen

and had also explained it to some freshmen
in his own science class.

He said the fact that he didn't even
teach biology—he teaches physics, math,

and general science—would probably
not come up in court, since the trial

was really more about the *idea*
than the instructor. As we talked,

I had to keep reminding myself that this
mild-mannered twenty-four-year-old teacher

was the target of every fundamentalist preacher
from here to the Mississippi. I asked him

if he felt like Joan of Arc, the French saint
whom they burned at the stake

for heresy. Scopes leaned back, stretched out
his long, skinny legs, scratched his head,

and said: "Well, maybe we are both
stubborn and maybe a little too

outspoken for our own good.
All the same, I doubt they'll set me aflame,

'cause they need me here next year
to coach their football team."

BETTY BARKER

I intercepted a young reporter
as he was leaving the sheriff's office
after interviewing
the devil-worshipping defendant
J. T. Scopes.

I filled him in on the real story:
"These atheist teachers have no
business bending the minds of our youth!

Their science books are written
by infidels
who want to turn our children away
from God."

I could tell by the way he shuffled in the dust
and scratched behind his neck
that he had not considered this
diabolical angle before.

"Ma'am, with all due respect," he said,
"I'm certain Mr. Scopes is not
in cahoots with the devil,
nor are the textbook editors, nor are any
other teachers I've met."

And I said, "There, you see . . . that black
magic is so powerful that even a smart
young man like you has been easily
taken in."

I gave him my full name and address
in case he wanted to quote me
in his paper.

MARYBETH DODD

It was a short third day in court.
The judge is still deciding
if the trial will go on
or if the Butler Act, which is a state law,
is unconstitutional,
which would mean that the charge
against Mr. Scopes should be
dropped.

Tillie gave me the afternoon free,
and while she drove off
in her jalopy,
I decided to hang around the Mansion.

I was dusting and straightening up
when Mr. Metcalf (he's a zoologist—
one of the seven men who got their picture taken)
invited me to sit and talk with him
and the others.

I was nervous at first . . . but do you know,
not one of them laughed at me
or left me out of their conversation.
When I got over my shyness, I asked
a question or two about zoology,
and another about anthropology,

and a few more about geology (those were
mostly for Pete—he really loves rocks).

Those seven professors talked and argued—
always in a friendly way, though—
right through the afternoon
and they let me sit right with them
and listen the whole time.

When Tillie got back, I had to
excuse myself to help her
in the kitchen.

We stood over the table
shucking corn,
shelling beans,
while Tillie rambled on about
her shopping trip to Morgan Springs.

I tried to listen.
But it was a lot less interesting than
stalactites,
tiger stripes,
and finding Neanderthals in frozen peat.

PART 5

A scientific soviet is attempting to dictate
what is being taught in our schools.
—William Jennings Bryan, prosecution lawyer

I sat speechless . . . a ringside observer at my
own trial, until the end of the circus.
—John T. Scopes, defendant

CONSTABLE FRAYBEL

As just about everyone expected,
the judge has ruled
the Butler Act is a fair law, which must
be respected.
So—the charges against Mr. Scopes
stand
and this trial will go on.

No surprise there.

No surprise either that after this week
of ninety-degree heat, no breeze,
and almost all the lawyers
and reporters in the chamber puffing
on a cigar or a cigarette, Judge Raulston
banged his gavel and boomed:
"No more smoking in the courtroom!"

When all the coughing stopped,

you could've heard
a pin drop.

Out of the corner of my eye, I saw
David Amos taking in some of the trial
with his son, Willy.
David was chewing slowly on a
plug of tobacco.

He nodded and grinned.

WILLY AMOS

Right after court got out
yesterday,
me and Pa drove our wagon straight
to the tobacco shack in Morgan Springs.
Pa traded the youngest of our mules
for three hundred plugs
of chewing tobacco.

On the courthouse lawn this mornin',
I sold every plug

at twice our buyin' price
'fore them doors even opened.

Good thing, too—'cause the
Dayton Entertainment Committee
had plenty more for me and Pa to do.
They paid us double time
to put more loudspeakers on the lawn
so that every visitor—
even if they're on the other end of town—
feels like they're right inside this Monkey Trial.

Soon as we were done,
Constable Fraybel called us in
'cause three of the electric fans
the judge had ordered to cool down the room
weren't workin'.

It took us most of the mornin', but me and Pa
fixed one fan, rigged the others
with chicken wire, then stuck around to see
if the constable'd be giving us
more jobs to do.

The judge was callin' in the jury,
startin' up court again, when I noticed
Mr. Scopes's lawyer, Mr. Neal,
lookin' all around the room for somethin'
or someone, somewhere . . .

Pa pointed to Mr. Scopes's chair, empty.

While we were fixin' those fans,
we'd heard J. T. Scopes
tell Mr. Bryan's son, W. J. Bryan *Jr.*,
that when court let out at noon,
he was goin' to sneak off to Millman's farm
for a quick swim in the pond
and Junior could come along.

"Get the wagon, Will," Pa said.

We hurried our mules up Market Street
out to Millman's pond,
where J. T. Scopes and W. J. Bryan Jr.
were neck-deep in water, laughin'
and splashin' like schoolkids.

"Hey, fellas!" Pa yelled.
"Come on outta there . . . trial's gonna
start again without ya!"

They came runnin' outta there
like a pair of snake-bit horses
and dried off best they could
while we drove 'em back to town.

"Thanks again," Scopes said, climbin' down
at the courthouse door.
"Though I'm not so sure I'm needed here!"

"Must be nice to be white," I said to Pa
when we'd pulled clear. "Seems you can be arrested
but you don't gotta go
to your own trial!"

CONSTABLE FRAYBEL

I've been doing most of my policing
outside, keeping the vendors,
self-proclaimed preachers, and, on occasion,
Betty's Bible study ladies
from blocking the path
to the courthouse door.

But today, I got a constable from Morgan Springs
to cover my sidewalk beat
while I took a seat
inside the Rhea County Courthouse
with all the other visitors, lawyers,
townsfolk, and reporters.

I wanted to listen as my
longtime pal and neighbor,
Walter White, the superintendent of schools

(and one of the five men whose plan
it was to bring this trial to town),
became the first prosecution witness,
the first man to take the stand
in the case of
Tennessee v. John Thomas Scopes.

And it was none too soon, either—
we were all starting to think the lawyers
would just keep arguing with each other
or with the judge,
and Dayton would be known
for holding the most *boring* trial in history!

Walter White came dressed in his best suit,
sat up straight, and smiled
for all the cameras.
He told the lawyers, judge, and jury
that Scopes admitted to discussing
evolution
in the classroom sometime in April,
and that he used
Hunter's *Civic Biology*,
which contained a section on evolution,
to conduct a science class review.

As I listened, I realized three things:

1. Walter White, as the superintendent
of schools, must have *approved* that textbook
before it could be used.

2. He also must have signed the contract
to hire J. T. Scopes as a science teacher.

3. He must have known that our good
friend Fred Robinson sells Hunter's
Civic Biology at his store, the very spot
where he and Walter White conspired
to have J. T. Scopes arrested for using it.

All I can say is:
the law is a fickle thing. I don't
pretend to understand it; I merely
enforce it.

PETER SYKES

Poor Howard Morgan! Just a little freshman.
Today he looked nervous and shy
when he took the stand to testify.

Howard had Mr. Scopes for general science
and sat in the front row the day they
talked about fossils, the formation of the

earth's layers, and the idea of evolution.
When the lawyers asked Howard's folks
if he would be a witness, they said *yes*,

but when the time came for him
to appear in court, the kid was scared
to say anything that might hurt his teacher.

Howard tried to hide in the woods,
but Mr. Scopes went and found him,
told him he should do his duty

and not be afraid, that he wouldn't
be mad at Howard no matter what he said.
Poor Howard Morgan . . . just a freshman.

Can't blame him, though. No one I know
wants to hurt Mr. Scopes (except maybe
W. J. Bryan and Miss Barker). Everyone

at school likes him. Everyone I know
wants to have him for science or math class
or to play for his football team.

I think it's strange that ever since this trial
began, all the grown-ups are falling
all over themselves to be seen

up front in court, and the kid (the one
the Butler Act is supposed to "protect")
wants nothing to do with it.

JIMMY LEE DAVIS

Pale as a
trout's belly.
That was
Howard Morgan
when he took
the stand today
in court.
He did pretty
good, though.
When he was
done, up comes
Bud Shelton,
a senior at
Rhea County High.
I made sure
I got off from
the store

so I could see
Bud testify
'cause the
Sheltons live
two houses
back of us
& I took his
sister to the
church social
last year.
Pete took off
& came to see
Bud too, but we
pretended we
didn't see each
other & I sat
close as
I could get
behind W. J. Bryan
& Pete sat
close as
he could get
to Mr. Darrow.

Here's how
it went: Attorney
General Stewart
asked Bud
if Mr. Scopes

used Hunter's
biology book
& if he told
the class anything
about evolution.
Bud said that
Scopes told them
how the earth
cooled
& single-celled
animals formed,
& how fish, birds,
& mammals—
*"and he told us
man was a mammal"*—
slowly evolved
from simpler
creatures &
adapted to their
environment.
Then it was
Darrow's turn:
"Did you stop
going to church
after that?" he
asked. Bud said:
"No, sir!" & then
Darrow asked:
"Did he teach you

anything else
that was wicked?"
& Bud answered:
"No, not that
I remember!"
A lot of folks
laughed at that.
Pete did, but
not me—Mr.
Darrow was
trying to make
evolution
seem harmless.
But it can't
be harmless if
it goes against
the Bible . . .
right?

PAUL LEBRUN

Special to the *St. Louis Post-Dispatch*

DAYTON, Tenn., July 15.—Today at the Scopes trial, two high school students (Howard Morgan, age fourteen, and Harry "Bud"

Shelton, age seventeen) were called as prosecution witnesses. There was some delay, however, as when lawyers summoned the younger one, he was nowhere to be found. Fearing his testimony might damage the reputation of his teacher, the young man had decided to run away. The defendant, J. T. Scopes—who, for some as yet undisclosed reason, arrived late to court this afternoon—took it upon himself to leave the courtroom to find the boy and bring him back.

During this short delay in what has so far been a highly unorthodox trial, W. J. Bryan once again seized the opportunity to give a speech. From his soapbox on the courthouse lawn, he declared to all who would listen (about seven hundred citizens by one estimate) that the very souls of their children were at stake in this debate, and they should stand fast in their literal belief in Genesis. During Bryan's speech, Clarence Darrow and his defense team strolled the main street, greeting townsfolk and sampling the local ice cream.

Scopes returned with the boy, who looked bedraggled and sheepish, and urged him to tell the truth about anything he was asked. Morgan and his older friend Shelton then took the stand one at a time, answering questions about evolution posed to them by the prosecution. Under oath, they told the court that Scopes had taught them "the earth was once a molten mass and that birds, insects, fish, and mammals had all started as single-cell organisms."

Afterward, outside the courthouse, Howard Morgan's mother shared her opinions on evolution. "It hasn't hurt me or my boy," she said. "I don't think any of us here in the mountains have studied evolution enough. I wish I knew more about it." Bud

Shelton's mother felt the same: "As far as I'm concerned, they can teach my boy evolution every day of the year," she declared. It seemed to her that the new idea had not affected her son very much, because "he had to get the [biology] book out and study it up for the trial."

Tomorrow, Clarence Darrow plans to bring in a string of witnesses (scientists and ministers) to prove that evolution does not contradict traditional religion but that each addresses a different aspect of humanity. Everyone in Dayton anticipates the first lengthy oratory by W. J. Bryan, as he will undoubtedly contest Darrow's witnesses. Day five of the Scopes Monkey Trial promises to be as intriguing as the four preceding.

WILLY AMOS

Clarence Darrow asks the right questions
at exactly the right time.

His witnesses were not
afraid of him; they were glad to speak
and to tell him
whatever he wanted to know.
Even the jury looked convinced!

Clarence Darrow uses words and ideas
like a boxer uses his fists—settin' up
the other lawyers just so,
then deliverin' the quick one-two
knockout blow.

I should know . . . I've had to get pretty good
at fightin' to protect myself
from the Klan-lovin' kids.

Lately, though, Dayton folks are too busy
with their own worries
to pay me much mind.
Standin' on the street corner, sellin' what I can,
I've heard my share of squabbles.
But I do reckon Mr. Darrow could argue
for just about anythin'
against just about anybody
and win.

Folks say he's defended
colored people, poor people, people who
had no one else to stand up for them.
Watchin' him, I got to wonderin'
if there will ever be
colored lawyers,
'cause maybe someday I might like to stand up for
colored people, red people, yellow people,
poor people, sick people.

Before he leaves town, I hope to ask
Mr. Clarence Darrow
what he thinks
about that.

MARYBETH DODD

The men who are staying at the Mansion
are being patient with our service,
minding their manners,
saying "please" and "thank you kindly, miss,"
and some of them, after dinner,
are even leaving tips!
(I finally told Daddy I was helping Tillie,
but I didn't tell him I was earning money.)

Everyone here says the trial will last
at least a few more days. That's *good*.
Already I've earned
four dollars and thirty-five cents,
which I've kept in a little tin box
in the bottom drawer of my dresser.

Late at night, when I hear Daddy snoring downstairs,
I tiptoe over there, pull out that drawer, open the lid
of that little tin box,
and just look at that money, thinking about
what I might do with it.

Perhaps this a sin. Probably it is.
I know Daddy would think so. He would remind me
to lay my treasures up in heaven
and not to covet
earthly goods.

But it's not goods I'm thinking of.
I'm wondering how much I will have to earn
for a train ticket to somewhere
I might see for myself
what the wider world has to offer
a small-town Tennessee girl
like me.

PAUL LEBRUN

One of the two reporters
in the room next to me

brought along his little Pekinese, which so far
has been a perfectly mannered companion,
quiet and (thankfully) housebroken.

"I covered that diphtheria story last January,"
the reporter told me. "The one where
that whole Alaskan town got sick
and the only thing standing between them
and death
was a team of hardy sled dogs
led by one particularly smart one."

"I remember reading about that," I said.
"Balto, right?"

"Yep, that's him. . . . I saw him once," he said.
"A husky. Looked just like a wolf, though.
And that whole team . . . like a pack of wolves.
They just loved that awful wind and ice and snow—
like it ran in their blood, you know?"

Then he laughed: "This pup here,
he'd lie down in the traces and howl for mercy.
He's made of different stuff
than his canine cousins."

I patted the little dog's head.
Charles Darwin, I thought, would have
enjoyed that story.

WILLY AMOS

Yesterday I was at my secret spot,
a small clearin' beyond the stand
of pines just outside of town
where once in a while I speak out loud to the trees
about my dreams
and nobody bothers me.

Yesterday I was not
Willy Amos, peddler of fruit and tobacco;
I was Willy Amos, lawyer for the defense,
fightin' against a big-city factory
forcin' its workers
to make twice as many gadgets
in half the time, payin' them
half the wages they should be makin',
and firin' them
if they made trouble.

I could see I was winnin' over the jury,
and I had the prosecution
tremblin', when someone stepped
into the clearin' behind me.

"Now look them straight in the eye,
tell them it's their sworn duty
to release your defendants,

people who are just like them:
hardworking, ethical, and innocent!"

I dropped the pine switch
I'd been wavin' and I looked
Mr. Clarence Darrow
straight in the eye while he waited
for my reply.

All those words
that'd come tumblin' from my mouth
so free and easy
now got stuck halfway up my throat.
I just stood there starin' . . . and all I could say was
absolutely nothin'.

MARYBETH DODD

Mr. Robinson sent Jimmy Lee Davis
to the Mansion
with some supplies for Tillie.

Jimmy Lee sat with me on the porch
while I shelled green beans

and he read to me from his copy of
the *Chattanooga Daily Times*.

"Get this, Marybeth—
out of the entire
five days this court
has been in session,
the jury has only
been in the room
for about two hours."

Two hours!
Why, in that same time I can shuck
a whole bushel of beans
or hem three pairs of Daddy's overalls.
I thought the jury was the most
important part of a trial.
Well—I guess not *this* trial . . .

"Says here Dr.
Maynard Metcalf
will testify
today—says he's
a zoologist from
Baltimore who
believes in God
& Jesus & in
evolution. He
sounds like a
liar to me!"

I tossed both halves of the green bean
I'd snapped
onto Jimmy Lee's lap.
"He's no liar," I said. "He's staying here
at the Mansion. He's one of the smartest
and one of the nicest men
I've ever met."

Jimmy Lee looked hurt.

"All right, all right—
I didn't mean nothing
by it. He just sounds
confused, that's all,
like he needs to
pick a side."

"Pick a side? Jimmy Lee, are you deaf?" I asked.
"Dr. Metcalf is a zoologist and a *Christian*—you just
read those words to me yourself. Can't he be both?"

"No, Marybeth.
Last time I checked,
Christians believed in
the Bible, which says
God created man
in his likeness
& the whole world
in seven days.

So how can he
be a Christian
& also believe
in evolution?"

Jimmy Lee sounded just like Daddy.
Made me so mad!

"I don't rightly know, but I think you can,"
I replied. "I think some people can look at a thing
a lot of different ways at once
and they can all be partly right."

Jimmy Lee looked at me like I had
two heads.

TILLIE STACKHOUSE

Now that Walter White, Howard Morgan,
and Bud Shelton
have all sworn in court
that J. T. Scopes did indeed teach evolution,
it's time to hear from
the defense.

The papers say Mr. Darrow plans
to put on the stand
as many scientists and ministers as he can
to show that devout, intelligent people—
and I have seven of them
staying here at the Mansion!—
can believe in both religion *and* evolution.

I decided I wanted to be there
when one of my best guests, Dr. Maynard Metcalf,
spoke his piece in court.

I sat with everyone else in that hotbox
of a room, as Dr. Metcalf, a zoologist
from Johns Hopkins University,
who believes absolutely in evolution—and who,
as a devout Christian and Sunday-school teacher,
believes absolutely in God—
explained Darwin's theory.

He said he believed it did *not* contradict
the Christian religion
but merely added another, more scientific dimension
to the story in Genesis. He said the term *evolution* means
"the whole series of physical changes
which have taken place
during hundreds of millions of years"
and which resulted in
"the change of an organism

from one character into a different character
[in terms of] its structure, or its behavior,
or its function."

Now, what I heard him say—by the *way* he answered
Mr. Darrow's questions—was:
man is both a spiritual and a physical being,
and religion (Genesis) and science (evolution)
deal with different parts
of human life.

Sadly, the jury heard none of it. Why?
Because Judge Raulston *excused* them!
Why, I wonder, did they bother to choose a jury
if they didn't mean to use them?

Of course, Attorney General Stewart
objected
to everything Metcalf said,
and called his testimony *irrelevant*.
The Butler Act, Mr. Stewart pointed out,
"outlawed any teaching about human evolution
regardless of what evolution meant
or whether it conflicted with the Bible."

Mr. Darrow replied
that according to the Butler Act,
Mr. Scopes was accused of teaching
a "theory that denies the story

of the Divine Creation of man,
as taught in the Bible," and that the defense
intended to show, with the testimony of
Dr. Metcalf and other scientists and ministers,
who were all Christians *and* evolutionists,
that Mr. Scopes did no such thing.

And that handsome, shy Mr. Scopes
just sat there quietly listening,
in case they needed him,
which it appears they don't,
while some of the smartest men in the country
tried to decide
exactly
what this trial is about.

PETER SYKES

Finally, Mr. William Jennings Bryan, the man
almost everyone has come to hear speak
(and he's been doing *plenty* of it outside of the court)—

finally, Mr. Bryan spoke: "Here is the book . . .
they used to teach your children!" he said,
holding up a diagram from *Civic Biology*.

"How dare those scientists put Man in
a little circle like that with all those animals
that have an odor! . . . [Surely] the parents
of this day have [a] right to declare
that children are not to be taught this."

Mr. Bryan rambled on for more than an hour,
arguing that the court had no business listening
to the testimonies of scientists; they just needed

to read their Bible and listen to their hearts.
After Mr. William Jennings Bryan spoke,
there was clapping and more clapping

and banging on chairs and just about
any kind of cheering you can imagine.
After Mr. Bryan sat down, Mr. Malone,

a defense lawyer, stood up. Our English teacher
would've liked what Mr. Malone said, because
for a New Yorker, he was pretty poetic:

"We have come here for this duel!" he cried.
"But does the opposition [believe] . . .
that we should be strapped to a board
and they alone should carry the sword?"

He meant, I guess, that if the judge did not
allow their expert witnesses, it would be like
making them face the enemy without a weapon.

It did seem mighty unfair to let the jury
hear all of the witnesses for one side
but none from the other. Mr. Malone looked

mad. But he stood his ground and declared
to the judge, the reporters, and the crowd:
"We feel we stand with fundamental freedom

in America. We are not afraid!" As soon as
Mr. Malone sat down, there was clapping
and more clapping and banging on chairs

and just about any kind of cheering you can imagine.
I heard one reporter say: "Now *this* is more like it!
This is what we came here to see!"

The judge adjourned and I got stuck on the stairway
for twenty minutes as everyone pushed and shoved
their way outside, and most of that time I was

smashed between two hillbillies and a sweaty,
chaw-loving lawyer, and I was thinking how
that diagram of man among all those smelly animals

was just about right.

MARYBETH DODD

One of the reporters
    staying at the Mansion
said he'd heard that a

nineteen-year-old girl
    from New York,
Gertrude Ederle, who won

three Olympic medals,
    will try to swim
across the English Channel

later this summer. No woman
    has ever made it,
though five men have,

and Gertrude Ederle says
    she'll do it in less time
and using a different stroke

(she calls it "the crawl")
    than any of the men.
They say the English Channel

is bitter cold, rough, and
    full of unpredictable currents—
waves that can knock you out

and ships that can run you
    down before you even
know what's happened.

Lord! And here I am thinking
    washing dishes and
waiting on tables is hard.

PETER SYKES

After court let out, I put in a few hours
back at the store. I swept the floor,
washed the soda counter, and unpacked

the last few boxes of ape masks.
"Pete, the place looks great," my boss said.
"I'm going home to check on Joe Mendi . . .

why don't you take a break?" Tired
and perspired, I sat at the counter
with a cold Coke and took out my

good-luck rock: a four-inch chunk
of white-and-black marble—
a Christmas gift from my uncle—

that came from a mountain near Knoxville,
right here in eastern Tennessee.
By now I must have looked at it

from every possible angle, every side,
and still I find new patterns every time.
And that is exactly what I was doing

when one of the men I recognized
as a defense witness at the trial
(one that's waiting to see if the judge

will let him testify) walked in.
"Could I get me one of those?" he asked
politely, pointing to my Coke.

"Yes, sir!" I replied, and jumped behind
the counter to pour him an extra-tall one.
He drank it down in less than a minute.

"This yours?" he asked, holding up my
lucky chunk of rock. "Yes, sir," I repeated.
"East Tennessee marble. I got a whole

collection at home: shale, granite, schist,
quartz, pumice, limestone, obsidian . . ."
He looked at me funny then.

I poured him a second one, on the house,
went in the back to wash my glass.
When I returned, he was gone.

On the counter, under my rock,
I found this note:

> *When you are through with high school,*
> *please come see me in my Nashville office.*
> *Enjoy the rest of your summer.*
>
> *Yours truly,*
> *W. A. Nelson,*
> *geologist for the State of Tennessee*

PAUL LEBRUN

Special to the *St. Louis Post-Dispatch*

DAYTON, Tenn., July 17.—It is the sixth day in the trial of *State of Tennessee v. John Thomas Scopes*. This morning, Judge Raulston read his decision regarding expert witnesses, which the defense maintains remain essential to the jury's understanding of the issues and to their own legal arguments on behalf of Mr. Scopes.

The judge has ruled against allowing any of the scientific or theological witnesses, assembled by Mr. Darrow and his associates, to testify in court. In his reading of the ruling, he appeared somewhat apologetic, perhaps a sign that he realizes how seriously this handicaps the defense. Two sources from the capitol in Nashville, who asked to remain anonymous, confirmed that "the judge has succumbed to pressure from state politicians to keep the trial short, and to try to minimize the mockery that has been hurled at his 'backwoods court' by several of the national newspapers."

After hearing the ruling, defense counsel Clarence Darrow immediately rushed to the bench and asked the judge to reconsider: "Has there ever been any effort to ascertain the truth in this case?" he exclaimed. The judge explained that he would allow Mr. Darrow and his team some time to prepare their witnesses' *written* statements, which would then be read into the court's official records—but would not be heard or read by the jury—in the event they would prove useful in an appeal.

When Darrow asked for the rest of the day to carry out this long and tedious task (the defense expects to record the testimony of more than a dozen witnesses), the judge did not comply. Mr. Darrow promptly exploded: "I do not understand why every request of the state and every suggestion of the prosecution should meet with an endless waste of time, and a bare suggestion on our part should be immediately overruled!" To which the judge replied: "I hope you do not mean to reflect upon the court!" It was obvious to everyone present that Mr. Darrow was indeed meaning to insult the court and, perhaps, after today's ruling, was justified in doing so. In the end, the judge acquiesced, adjourning the session to give Darrow and his team the rest of the afternoon to record their witnesses' statements.

With this final announcement, a long week of religious rants and legal details has drawn to a comparatively quiet close. Several of the local lawyers believe that when court reconvenes on Monday, Raulston will charge Darrow with contempt for challenging his ruling in such an unprofessional manner. Given the unrelenting heat here in Dayton (some fundamentalists claim it's the proximity of Satan himself), you can be sure that those who choose to spend their weekend debating Darwinism will stay far away from the stifling confines of the Rhea County Courthouse.

CONSTABLE FRAYBEL

Judge Raulston has handed down his decision
not to allow
more scientists or ministers to appear
as witnesses,
but he *did* allow the defense the rest of
the day to make
a written record of what their witnesses
would have said

and what the defense had *wanted* to prove before
he ruled against it.

To me, the judge's decision seemed
ridiculous.
Most of us here in Dayton wanted to hear more
about evolution . . .
and not just from the scientists' point of view,
but from the ministers' too.

Darrow claims his witnesses believe in the Bible
and in Darwin;
he claims they are anxious to explain the difference
between science and religious faith
and how they made places in their hearts and minds
for both.

Not allowing those witnesses to speak is like announcing
a big football game,
telling folks from all around to come and see
who will win,
but then the referee lets only *half* the visiting team
onto the field,
and the coach has to explain how the game
would have been played
if he'd been allowed to use his whole team!

I never went to law school. But I *have* played
some football . . .

and if this were a County High game
and Judge Raulston
was the referee, I believe they'd run him
clear out of Tennessee.

PART 6

William Jennings Bryan: "Your Honor . . . The only purpose Mr. Darrow has is to slur at the Bible, but I will answer his questions."

Clarence Darrow: "I object to your statement. I am examining you on your fool ideas that no intelligent Christian on earth believes."

BETTY BARKER

At our Bible study, we gave thanks
for Judge Raulston, that he found strength

to make the right decision, that he did not allow
any of Darrow's scientific witnesses

or any Darwin-believing ministers
(more of Satan's messengers in disguise!)

to testify at our trial. When our time was
through, I held up a copy of

The Great Gatsby, which I took upon myself
to confiscate from our town library.

In Mr. Fitzgerald's book, you can find
every sin of this latest generation—

its love of good times, easy living,
wild parties with lustful dancing

and too much drinking. I held it
high so everyone could see.

Then I tossed it to the ground,
lit a match, and watched it burn, just as

all the sinners who read it will burn
if they do not turn and repent!

TILLIE STACKHOUSE

I received another batch of cookies
and a letter from my sister:

> *Dear Tillie,*
>
> *You should know that the* New York Times
> *keeps our city well informed*
> *about your trial.*
> *Today, on the front page, they printed*
> *every word*
> *that Mr. Bryan and Mr. Malone said*
> *in their debate about those "expert witnesses."*
>
> *Everyone here in New York*
> *is talking about it—*

teachers, bankers, plumbers, street
vendors, waitresses, and chimney sweeps . . .
everyone is guessing what the effect will be
if the jury in Tennessee
finds J. T. Scopes guilty.

Dearest Tillie, please excuse the brevity
of this letter. . . . You see, I have been
invited to a reading this evening
at the New York Public Library,
where author F. Scott Fitzgerald
will read from The Great Gatsby!

I must go now and get ready—
enjoy the cookies.

Your loving sister,
Lila

MARYBETH DODD

I got Tillie in a quiet moment
when she was reading
Darwin's book
and sampling her sister's cookies.

I asked if I might use
the address for the Mansion as if
it were my own,
so I could send away for something
I didn't want Daddy to see
at home.

Tillie, I could tell, wanted—
in the worst way—
to ask me what I was sending for,
but instead
all she said was:
"Sure."

WILLY AMOS

"Good thing we struck while the iron was hot!"
That's what Pa said. He meant
we were lucky to get
the money we got
while the scientists, preachers, press,
and thrill-seekers were in town.

Now it's Saturday, July 18,
and even though the trial is still goin' on

(they start up again on Monday)
most of our visitors are leavin'.

"Can't blame 'em," Pa said.
"Since the judge ruled against
all
of Mr. Darrow's defense witnesses
there ain't no reason to stay."

This mornin', me and Pa helped two men
from radio station WGN
take down their microphones and metal stands.
One of 'em was friendly enough, so I
asked him what he thought
would happen Monday in court.

"Well . . . since Darrow's got no witnesses
left, Mr. Scopes has no defense," he said.
"I guess the jury will say he's guilty
and the judge will fine him,
and that'll be the end of it!"

"You ain't stayin' for that?" I asked.

"Nah—nothing exciting's going to happen,"
he replied, wipin' the sweat off his neck.
"We're heading back to Chicago,
where at least there's a breeze. . . .
We'll just read about it in the papers
like everyone else."

I bet he thought since I'm colored,
I would have to ask
someone else
to read the paper for me.
And he'd be wrong.

PAUL LEBRUN

Acid-tongued, quick-spoken
H. L. Mencken.
He's the most famous reporter covering
this trial—and the most opinionated.
I've heard that he's slurred
this town, this state, these kind, hardworking people
in almost every article he's written
for the *Baltimore Sun*.

Today, at Robinson's soda fountain,
I heard that Mencken
is planning to leave Dayton
because he feels these legal proceedings—
or at least the important parts—
are mostly over. But Mrs. Stackhouse
told me he's leaving for another reason:

"Some of the locals have threatened
to do him harm
on account of his making them look like
ignorant,
  backwoods,
    Bible-thumping
      hicks
in his newspaper articles."

I believe her. Mencken is well known
for his satire,
but I think he's been a bit unfair
to the people in Dayton.

So it's probably wise of him to go,
and though many more reporters from the
big-city papers are going home, too,
I have decided to stay
at least until Monday, on a hunch
that there might be something important
to report.
Call it instinct . . . I don't know.
My boss will say, "Lebrun! Get back here.
This trial's already cost me too much dough!"

But sure as cows can smell rain,
I am praying
that my second long, hot weekend in Dayton
will not be in vain.

JIMMY LEE DAVIS

The Lord works in
mysterious ways.

Today, as a favor to
Mrs. Stackhouse, I
took one of her guests
out to the trout stream
so he could try some
Tennessee fly fishing
before he left. Turns out
he was Mr. Metcalf,
one of the scientists
who came to testify
for the defense, but
who the judge said
couldn't. (Tarnation!
If Jesus hadn't said,
"Love your enemies,"
I'd have found
someone else to
take him fishing!)
I led him to the stream,
but not to the *best* spot.
We cast our lines &
I kept quiet. "You believe
in evolution, son?" he asked

me all of a sudden. "Don't
know," I replied. "I do
believe in Jesus, though."
"So do I," he said. "No
need to give up your
faith just because of
Darwin." We cast a
few more times
but reeled in our lines,
empty. It was hot
even in the shade,
so we sat on the bank
& shared some lemonade.
"I don't really get,"
I confessed, "how you
can believe in two
different things. . . ."

He thought about this.

"You take physics?"
he asked. I told him
I did. "Then you know
that when you hear
Al Jolson on the radio
or 'Silent Night' on
the church organ that
sound waves are coming
off their instruments

& traveling into your
ears, right?" I told him
yes, we learned that
last year. "Well, since
you learned that, did
you stop listening to
music? Do you love
those tunes any less
when you hear them?"

I thought about this.

We shared a second
glass & talked some
more about school
& about Jesus, too.
"Let's move down the
stream a bit," I said
when he picked up
his reel again. "I have
a hunch we'll have
better luck there. . . ."

PAUL LEBRUN

As someone who makes a literary living,
I have always appreciated
irony.

So when I asked the young waitress at the Mansion
where I might find a clothing store,
and she replied: "That would be Darwin's,"
I gave her the strangest look.

"Really, sir, that's the owner's name:
J. R. Darwin"—
and she pointed me down the street.

I found Darwin's place not far from
Robinson's Drugs, which was open late
and still doing a brisk business
selling Simian Sodas
and fold-out paper apes.

J. R. Darwin himself helped me choose
a new pair of trousers, a vest,
and two button-down shirts
to replace the ones I'd ruined
in that sweaty, overstuffed courtroom.

"So, Mr. Darwin," I asked before I left,
"do you believe in survival of the fittest?"

A good-natured man, Darwin laughed
and patted me on the back.
"Son, I make my living making sure
things fit . . . but I have to live in this town
after you leave, so don't go
spreading that around!"

"Your secret's safe with me," I said.
Then I walked out onto Market Street
and saw Robinson's monkey
dressed in a vest
just like mine.

JIMMY LEE DAVIS

After I brought
Mr. Metcalf
back to the Mansion,
I headed to the
store for my
weekly pay.
On the way,
I found this
weird rock—
like a diamond
only pink—
& I put it in
my pocket.
At Robinson's,
Pete was working
the soda fountain
but the boss
was out. I sat
down to wait
till he came back.

"Marybeth told me
you been fishing,"
Pete said finally,
breaking the silence.
"Any luck?"

"Yep. Four trout
& a pickerel," I replied.
Pete nodded. "Nice."
I put the pink rock
on the counter.
"You want this
for your collection?"
Pete wiped his
hands & picked
it up.
"Rose quartz—a real
clean piece. Thanks!"
He turned on the
radio. The Yanks
were playing &
Lou Gehrig was up.
He took two pitches,
then hit a long ball
down the right-field
line. Two runs scored
& Gehrig held up
at second. "Wahoo!
Loouuuuu!"
we yelled. I jumped
off my stool so me
& Pete could do our
celebration dance,
just like always.

ERNEST McMANUS

I stood beside the constable
in the town park
while W. J. Bryan and Clarence Darrow
made their weekend statements
to the members of the press
who hadn't left.

As usual, Mr. Bryan clearly enjoyed
his chance to speak
and to call Mr. Darrow
an anti-Christian conspirator:

> "The Tennessee case has uncovered
> the conspiracy against the Bible . . .
> the Christian world is not going
> to give up!"

All around us, people applauded.

Then Mr. Darrow replied:

> "I have no desire to have the Christian world
> give up its belief . . . but a very large portion
> of the Christian world do not regard the
> Bible as a book of science!"

Again, there was applause—
from some of the very same people.

After the crowd dispersed, the constable
invited me to walk over
to Robinson's for sodas.

"You know," I confessed to him, "I'm rooting
for Darrow, but I wish Bryan
wasn't so great at speaking!"

The constable shook his head. "Well, I'm
trying to stay behind Mr. Bryan . . .
but I wish Darrow
didn't make so much sense!"

PETER SYKES

Me and Jimmy Lee stowed our fishing poles
back behind the church. Soon as the minister
said the last amen, we hightailed it up

to Connor's Pond. Jimmy Lee told me about
taking Mr. Metcalf fishing, and I told him
I was sweet on Marybeth Dodd. I said I

thought he might be sweet on her, too,
'cause I saw them sitting together, talking,
on the Mansion steps. "Naw—she don't

like me, Pete. Thinks I'm hard of hearing, too!"
Jimmy said. But he laughed about it,
so I figured whatever Marybeth said,

he'd forgiven her. "She has a temper,
that girl," Jimmy said. "Maybe you
& me should practice fighting more

if you plan to date her!" We spent
the whole rest of the day at the pond.
Didn't catch much—didn't care.

MARYBETH DODD

"Why should we be afraid of new ideas?
If we always did everything the old way,

we'd be walking instead of driving
Tillie's jalopy to Morgan Springs—

we'd still have to eat by candlelight
and women couldn't vote!"

That's what I told Daddy
after we'd listened to Reverend Morris

go on and on and on and on
this morning at the Sunday service

about "the evils of this modern age."
And do you know what Daddy said?

"We were all better off when
women knew their rightful place.

Now that you got the vote, you girls believe
you can put your finger into every pot—

taste a little of whatever you please.
But that's not the Christian woman's way."

So I said: "Does the Bible forbid women
to think? Does it say we are just

pretty pets to be tied up or dragged around
on leashes, waiting for the next kind word

or crumb of food from our master?"
He looked like he'd been shot when I said that,

but I was mad, so I went on: "Daddy, in case
you forgot, I am seventeen. In four years,

I can vote—and I *will* vote 'cause I have my own
ideas and opinions about the way this country

should be run. Why should I have to stand still
and watch the world go by when you know

I'm smarter than most of the boys
at County High? Somewhere over those hills,

there's a whole world full of opportunity
for a girl like me. And someday, no matter what

you say, I'm going to see what's out there,
see what I can really do." We were back home

by then. I ran in, slammed the door to my room.
From my window, I saw him pacing back

and forth beneath the cherry tree, running
his hands through his hair and looking

for all the world like a confused little boy.

BETTY BARKER

Most of the infidels have left.
Seems there was not enough
wickedness to sustain their interest.

Seems the folks here in Tennessee
were too close to their Lord
to afford more public scrutiny.

Today is Sunday, a day of rest
and prayer. Then, in court on Monday,
the jury will most certainly

pronounce that atheist teacher guilty
and we Christians will have
our long-awaited victory.

PART 7

Shut the door to science when science sets
a canker on the soul of a child.

—Thomas Stewart, attorney general
for the State of Tennessee

I do not think about things I don't think about.

—William Jennings Bryan, prosecution lawyer,
in response to Darrow's questions on human history

PAUL LEBRUN

I rose before dawn after a sound sleep
in the quiet, half-empty Mansion.
I dressed quickly
in my new J. R. Darwin suit
and made some notes for what might be
the last full day of this trial.

Funny . . . there's a part of me
that can't wait to get back to St. Louis:
city lights, wide sidewalks, my own desk
and bed. Heck, I've even missed
my grouchy, perfectionist boss!

But there's another part of me
that doesn't want to leave this town
with its simple hospitality,
its glorious songbird mornings,
its loyal, lovable people.

Downstairs, Mrs. Stackhouse
and her young cousin, Miss Dodd,
greeted me warmly
with a four-inch pile of flapjacks
and strawberry jam.
I worked my way through that
delectable stack,
wondering what I could do
to pay them back,
show them my appreciation.

As I was eating, I was glancing
over all the vacated tables . . .
when it came to me.
"Ladies!" I said, pushing away my scraped-clean
plate. "I imagine,
now that most of the press have left,
those front-row reporters-only seats
at the courthouse will be pretty empty.
Would you be interested
in sitting up there with me
for today's proceedings?"

MARYBETH DODD

The reporter from the *St. Louis Post-Dispatch*
(Tillie says he's twenty-three,
but he doesn't look a day older than me)
invited both of us to join him
up front
at the vacated reporters' tables
for what he thinks might be
the last day of this trial.

When I asked him why he stayed
while almost everyone else left,
he said: "I have a hunch. . . ."

After the opening prayer, the first thing
Judge Raulston did was to charge Mr. Darrow
with contempt
for his angry outburst in the courtroom
on Friday.

Mr. Darrow, who probably expected that,
came prepared. He made a big
public apology to Judge Raulston.

The judge withdrew his charge.

Next, Mr. Darrow's defense lawyers
objected

to the huge sign saying READ YOUR BIBLE
that Betty Barker and her Bible study ladies
had erected
right beside the building
in full sight of the jury.

The lawyers demanded one of two things:
    1. a sign saying READ YOUR EVOLUTION
    should be posted next to it
    Or . . .
    2. the READ YOUR BIBLE sign
    should be taken down.

The judge ordered that sign removed, casting
a quick warning look at Betty Barker,
who squirmed and stamped
but for a change
kept her mouth shut.

Then someone came in and handed
the judge a note, which he read to himself,
then very quickly announced
that the floor of the courtroom
was showing signs of weakening
(new cracks downstairs in the ceiling)
from holding the weight of all those people
and all that equipment last week,
and the rest of the day's proceedings
would take place on the lawn.

As we filed outside, I told Mr. Lebrun:
"Good thing you stayed—there's plenty
to write about."

He grinned and took my arm.
"Miss Dodd, I have a feeling
there's much more to come."

JIMMY LEE DAVIS

Monday morning
at Robinson's store
was about as interesting
as watching grass grow.

I scrubbed the soda
counter & washed
all the glasses. Pete
swept the floor,
folded up some
packing boxes,
& taped the last

monkey mask to
the front door.
While our boss
counted cash
at the register,
I daydreamed I was
at the stream,
reeling in a twenty-
pound bass . . .
when a man came
rushing in
from the street:
"Trial's moved
outside!" he cried.
"Rumor has it
Darrow's got
one witness
the judge can't
refuse!"
I looked over
at Pete & he
looked up at me
& we both turned
to Mr. Robinson,
who shut the register,
took down the
OPEN sign,
& grabbed his hat.
"You boys coming?"
he asked, which—

with all due respect—
was a pretty
stupid question.

ERNEST McMANUS

Shocked. Flabbergasted. Stunned.

That was how I'd describe
the look on everyone's face
when Mr. Hays stood next to the little table
where he and Mr. Darrow sat serenely
on the courthouse lawn and said:
"The defense calls Mr. William Jennings Bryan
to the stand!"

The lawyers for the prosecution looked
horrified. Tongue-tied. Stupefied.

Except for Mr. Bryan, that is. . . .
It took him about two seconds
to jump into
the witness chair.

He knew he had finally been given
the spotlight he craved
and he was eager to use it.

Attorney General Stewart,
when he had shaken off his shock,
got right to his feet
and objected.
But Mr. Bryan silenced him. He was ready
to prove
that he could hold his own with Clarence Darrow
and to put
the evil evolutionists
in their place.

PETER SYKES

In case Mr. Bryan changed his mind
about testifying (doesn't look that way),
Mr. Darrow wasted no time getting started.

Mr. Darrow asked Mr. Bryan many
different questions about the Bible,
including if he truly believed that Jonah

lived for three days in the belly of a whale
and at the end of that time "the whale
spit him back onto the land, unharmed."

I figured Mr. Bryan would say, "Well, it may
not have happened *exactly* that way . . . ,"
but instead Mr. Bryan said: "I believe in

a God who can make a whale and can
make a man, and make *both* do what He pleases!"
As he talked I was thinking: Jeez . . . I am a believer

in the Bible and the teachings of Jesus;
but I also grew up in east Tennessee,
and like most folks here, I have

a kind of respect for how a story
grows with the telling. It's like when
my mother says, "Pete—if you pick up

one more rock, I swear, I'll make you
carry them all back up that mountain
and put them where they belong!"

Now, I know when she says that,
she *really* means I need to clean my room
so my clothes and schoolbooks

are more obvious than my favorite
chunks of granite. And that's the best way
I can explain how I thought about

that Jonah-in-the-whale Bible tale, ever
since we learned it in Sunday school. I never
did truly believe that a whale could eat

a human being and spit him back out,
unharmed and alive, three days later.
I figure God is a lot like my mother:

when she wants me to listen up
about something important, a little
exaggeration often works best.

WILLY AMOS

I could hardly believe it.
There I was, whittlin' a stick
on the side lawn of the courthouse,
countin' in my head
how many more fans I was

needin' to sell so I could buy
that winter coat
in the window at Morgan Springs.

I was figurin' twenty-four, twenty-five . . .
when here comes everyone
through them doors, back outside!

The constable waved me over.
Me and Pa helped him set up tables
for the lawyers and reporters
in the shade of the big maples.

When everyone got settled again,
Mr. Darrow called
Mr. Bryan to the stand,
and started firin' questions.

This went on for a while,
with Darrow askin' about all kinds of writin's
in the Bible (I knew most of them, too!),
but then he caught Mr. Bryan
in a trap
by askin' him if he believed that
everythin' and everyone
on earth
was wiped out after the Great Flood,
just like it says in the verses.

Mr. Bryan said he thought that was right,
'cept "the fish may have lived."

Everyone laughed hard at that,
includin' Mr. Darrow. Mr. Bryan added
that he had figured out when
the Great Flood actually was:
4,273 years ago.

No one laughed then. Almost everyone
looked impressed.

TILLIE STACKHOUSE

Mr. Bryan sure knew his Bible.
I'll bet even Betty Barker
hadn't gone to the trouble to figure out
when the Great Flood was.

But right after that, Darrow asked
if Mr. Bryan was familiar
with the ancient civilizations
of China and Egypt, where people lived

more than six thousand or seven thousand years ago,
with no evidence of interruption
by a Great Flood.
(A good strategy, I thought . . . Mr. Darrow
was trying to show
that the flood story was a Bible tale,
and that maybe there *was*
a certain flood in a certain place,
but that it was not meant to be taken
literally as world history.)

Mr. Bryan said he was not familiar
with those ancient folk—
said he'd never read about them.

"You have never in all your life
made any attempt to find out about the
other peoples of the earth?" Mr. Darrow asked.
"You don't care how old the earth is—
how old Man is,
how long the animals have been here?"

"I am not so much interested in that,"
Mr. Bryan replied.

I leaned over and whispered to Mr. Lebrun:
"I'll bet you don't get to ignore
world events just 'cause
they don't interest you."

"No, ma'am," he replied. "I surely do not!"

MARYBETH DODD

Nearly everyone in Dayton was standing
on the lawn of the courthouse

trying to get the best view of Mr. Bryan
and Mr. Darrow as they began their

"duel to the death." Mr. Darrow asked:
"Do you claim that everything in the Bible

should be literally interpreted?" Mr. Bryan
shouted: "I believe everything in the Bible

should be accepted as it is given there."
Across the sea of hats and palm-leaf fans

I saw Jimmy Lee and Pete standing with
their boss underneath a tree—I wanted Pete

to see me, but with that big crowd between us,
I don't think he could. Anyway . . . Mr. Darrow

asked Mr. Bryan a lot of questions about Jonah
and the whale, Adam and Eve, Noah and the Flood.

But to me, the most important one he asked was:
"Do you believe the sun was made on the

fourth day?" Mr. Bryan said yes, but he
couldn't explain how there were three "days"

and three "nights" before that. Then Mr. Bryan said
that maybe, just maybe, those "days" were actually

"periods," and maybe those periods
were actually millions of years!

There was a ripple of whispers
through the crowd. Tillie elbowed me.

"He just admitted that Genesis might not need
to be read literally!" she whispered.

"That means Mr. Scopes isn't guilty?" I asked.
Tillie shook her head. "No. I think they'll say

he is. . . . But if Mr. Bryan keeps contradicting
himself, there won't be one intelligent person

in Tennessee who will believe it!"

CONSTABLE FRAYBEL

As the afternoon wore on,
there were a lot more people on the lawn
watching and listening to
Darrow and Bryan
as they sparred and argued.

Then, all of a sudden,
like watching wild turkeys bursting from the brush,
things got hot—real hot.

After Darrow questioned Bryan
about certain ancient people,
it appeared he'd revealed to everyone present,
about a thousand, I'd say,
just how little Bryan knew, or even cared,
about history outside the Bible.

It appeared that even Bryan himself
realized

that Darrow had made him look foolish.
So—he got mad. Real mad.

"Atheist!" he shouted at his former friend.

"Bigot!" Darrow shot back.

The two men stood and shook their
fists at each other.

"Agnostic!" Bryan continued.

"Ignoramus!" Darrow countered.

The crowd started shifting—
and there was cheering and booing and hissing.
People jostled for a better view
of the two lawyers,
who continued their bitter quarrel
like they were a couple of roosters
strutting and squabbling
over a hen.

I waited to see if I'd be needed
to break up any fights,
but it was clear that only those two in suits
were being unruly—
and that was the bailiff's territory.

I moved over to a larger patch of shade,
where I stood with Fred Robinson.

"You should have brought Joe Mendi along,"
I said. "He'd fit right in with the rest of these
well-dressed beasts."

ERNEST McMANUS

When Darrow and Bryan had reached the peak
of their shouting and name-calling,
when there was both cheering and booing
from the crowd,
the judge banged his gavel loudly
and adjourned quickly.

I left that contentious scene,
walked to the other end of Market Street,
to seek the quiet
of the Mansion's garden.

After a while, a few reporters arrived
and went immediately upstairs
to their rooms.

A hush fell over the town.
Even the bees seemed to sleep.
The only sound to pierce the calm
was the gentle tapping of fingers
on typewriter keys,
which floated down to me
as I strolled among geraniums and roses.

I imagined the monks of medieval nights
seated at tables
in their damp scriptorium
scribbling away by the dim light
of candles, trying to communicate
the true magnitude of God's glory,
but also trying to respect the fact
that they alone,
at the bidding of the Church,
were the only ones permitted
literacy,
and that whatever they wrote
would be taken as truth . . .
and what, after all,
was truth
but what the heart believed
and what the mind perceived,
and how in the world
could they do justice
to both?

PAUL LEBRUN

Special to the *St. Louis Post-Dispatch*

DAYTON, Tenn., July 20.—On this seventh day of the Scopes trial, there was more pure emotion than on any day before. The trial began inside and ended outside (still in sweltering heat) as a safety precaution due to an unreliable floor. On the courthouse lawn, Darrow and Bryan dueled verbally over their interpretations of human history as the ever-growing crowd cheered and jeered and cooled themselves with fans, watching the kind of intense and impassioned debate between these two giants that they had all been waiting for.

Judge Raulston, in a change from previous days, allowed the jury to remain present, for which they appeared exceedingly grateful. Defense attorney Clarence Darrow relied on his own knowledge of the Bible as a basis for his questioning of W. J. Bryan, whom he called to the witness stand despite the objections from the rest of the prosecution. Darrow asked Bryan about Bible passages including the seven-day creation story found in Genesis, Jonah and the whale, and the Great Flood. Darrow asked Bryan about specific aspects of these accounts and whether they should be taken literally (a man living for three days in the belly of a whale, for instance) even if they contradicted well-established fact.

Darrow was clearly on his game, and after a short time Bryan was clearly flustered. Careful not to attack the Bible as an instrument of faith, but only to show it as an inappropriate source of science,

Darrow successfully exposed the limits of Genesis in depicting the facts of early human history. By the end of his interrogation, Bryan appeared infuriated. The two men finished the day in a shouting match over which the adjournment was barely heard.

Now this trial is drawing to a close. Darrow's final move—putting the leading man from the prosecution on the witness stand—seems to have been effective, at least in the short run. It remains to be seen, however, what the judge will say tomorrow. Meanwhile, the peach trees and blueberry bushes are at peak season and there's hay to be brought in. "Most of them jury men need to get back to their farms quick as they can!" one local man told me. Another reason to believe this Monkey Trial is almost over.

TILLIE STACKHOUSE

Hard to imagine . . .

those two men who stood up on the courthouse lawn
and faced each other,
shouted
and called each other names,

hard to imagine
they both sat, just a week ago, on the front porch
of the Mansion, after having dinner
together,

and reminisced about politics,
while we enjoyed their frequent
laughter
from inside the kitchen,

and tried to keep the pans and kettles
quiet
so we could listen to their good-natured
intelligent chatter.

CONSTABLE FRAYBEL

A light rain fell
on my shoulders as I walked
down Market Street.

Judge won't be holding court
on the lawn today, I thought.

And I was right.

Judge Raulston ordered me
to stand outside the main courthouse door
and let some folks in, but turn the rest
away, to prevent more
c r a c k s
in the unreliable floor.

PETER SYKES

Mr. Robinson didn't bother
to open his store this morning.
It was raining a little,

so the trial moved back inside,
where Jimmy Lee and I easily found
two seats near the front.

After seeing those two lawyers
going at each other like
wild tomcats, me and Jimmy Lee

felt even worse about our own fight
over this Monkey Trial. Like us,
Darrow and Bryan had once been

good friends. It was like watching
ourselves up there duking it out,
and it was darned *embarrassing*.

After that, we made a pact
not to let anything that might happen
at this trial come between us.

Judge Raulston's still worried about
this floor—he had Constable Fraybel
making sure there weren't too many
people crowding in like before.
(But we got to laughing at the clever ones
sneaking through the back door!)

The judge called the court to order.
He made it clear straight off
that nothing Mr. Darrow or Mr. Bryan

had said yesterday out on the lawn
should be considered by the jury, and
that Mr. Darrow would not be allowed

to question Mr. Bryan anymore.
I asked a reporter who was sitting
close to us why Mr. Darrow wasn't hopping

mad about that. "Darrow proved his point.
He doesn't need to question Bryan
further," he explained. Obviously,

that reporter knew what he was
talking about, 'cause right then
Mr. Darrow got to his feet: "I think

to save time, we will ask the court
to bring in the jury and instruct the jury
to find the defendant guilty," he said.

I sat there thinking I should understand why
Mr. Darrow said this, but I really didn't.
Neither did Jimmy. This time, Jimmy asked.

"That way, Darrow can appeal the case
to a higher court," the reporter whispered.
"Hey! Aren't you the kid who tried to sell me

a stuffed monkey?" Jimmy nodded. "Yes, sir.
That was me all right. But you're too late now,"
he whispered as the guy tried to listen

and write at the same time. "We're all
sold out!" The reporter didn't seem
too terribly disappointed.

WILLY AMOS

Eight days.
That's how long this trial's gone on.

Nine minutes.
That's how long it took the jury
to reach a verdict
in the case of *Tennessee v. John Thomas Scopes*.

Me and Pa arrived in time
to watch those twelve men walk out
and walk back in again
so their foreman could say:
"We have found the defendant
guilty!"

Judge Raulston asked Mr. Scopes
to approach the bench
so that he could assign the fine
of one hundred dollars,
payable to the clerk,

in cash or personal check.

PAUL LEBRUN

Special to the *St. Louis Post-Dispatch*

DAYTON, Tenn., July 21.—The Dayton trial concluded today in rather undramatic fashion. After first establishing that there would be no further questioning of W. J. Bryan by Clarence Darrow or by any other member of the defense, the judge ruled that any testimony given by Mr. Bryan while he was on the stand Monday would not be considered. Mr. Darrow, having nothing further to offer in defense of J. T. Scopes (who stands accused of teaching evolution despite the Tennessee law that forbids him to do so), asked the jury to return a verdict of guilty. This would allow him to appeal this case to a higher and, one would imagine, less biased court.

When the foreman announced the guilty verdict, there was hardly any reaction in the courtroom. After the judge disallowed all of the defense witnesses and further ordered the jury to disregard everything W. J. Bryan had said yesterday while on the stand, there could hardly be a different result. The judge then permitted John Thomas Scopes a moment to express his thoughts. As this was the first time during the entire eight-day trial that the defendant's own voice was heard, I give you here that speech in its entirety:

> "Your Honor, I feel that I have been convicted of violating an unjust statute. I will continue in the future, as I have in the past, to oppose the law in any way I can. Any other action would be in violation of my ideal of academic

> freedom—that is, to teach the truth as guaranteed in our Constitution, of personal and religious freedom. I think the fine is unjust."

After Scopes spoke, a spontaneous burst of applause broke out among the high school students who had attended some of the trial. However, one local woman, who has been quite a vocal anti-evolutionist, had to be removed from the room as she prepared to hurl her handbag at Scopes.

After brief statements from the prosecution and the defense, in which they expressed gratitude to the townspeople for their kind hospitality, court was adjourned. The judge admonished everyone to keep moving while exiting, as the crack in the courthouse floor had not yet been repaired.

PART 8

[It was] a drugstore discussion that got past control.

—J. T. Scopes, defendant, describing the Dayton trial

If I should die tomorrow, I believe that on the basis of the accomplishments of the last few weeks, I could truthfully say, *well done*.

—William Jennings Bryan's comments to a journalist, July 25, 1925

MARYBETH DODD

The Mansion's quiet now.
Most everyone's left for the train
that will take them back to
Chicago, Baltimore, New York, Boston.

I'd been dreading this time . . .
the long hours of washing linen,
stacking dishes, storing leftover food.
As I worked, I daydreamed a little—

thinking about how much I liked it
when Pete came by to help . . . his
smile, his voice, his easy way of talking.
I hoped he'd come by again soon.

By five o'clock, I started thinking about
getting home, having a cold glass of
lemonade, putting my feet up to read.
Closing the cupboards, I heard Tillie

call to me from the other room.
"This came for you," she said, handing me
a letter addressed to the Mansion from
"Admissions, University of Tennessee."

Tillie was grinning like Alice's Cheshire Cat.
"When I asked to use this address, did you
know I was sending for this?" I asked.
"No. No, I didn't . . . that's a fact. I knew you

were smart, Marybeth, but I didn't think
you'd have the nerve, with the way your
daddy can be, to do this yourself." She walked
over to the high corner shelf and pulled

down a box. "So I sent away for these. . . ."
Inside, I found applications for three more
colleges in the South and one in New York.
I threw my arms around Tillie, hugged her

like I would my own mother if she were alive.
She got all teary-eyed and shy. "Shucks,"
she sniffed. "This trial's brought me more
good hugs than I've had in quite a while!"

TILLIE STACKHOUSE

I sent Marybeth
off on an errand for the Mansion
to buy me a little
time . . . then I took a half dozen
of Lila's sugar cookies
up to my cousin Frank's
and sat out on the porch, waitin'.

"I know why you're here, Tillie,"
Frank said when he finally came outside.
"And it's no use."

I felt my anger rising right up in my throat.
I opened my mouth to tell him—
in so many words—
that he had no right to hold
that girl back, no cause to be afraid
that he'd lose her forever
if he let her out of Dayton.

But I didn't have to say even
one word.

My hardheaded, soft-hearted cousin Frank
sat down next to me and said: "Can you
forgive this old fool?"

I gave him the biggest cookie and assured him
I could.

JIMMY LEE DAVIS

Mr. Robinson
gave us each
a bonus, told us
he'd never had
such good workers
in his store before.
It *was* kind of fun,
but I'm glad this
trial is done so
things can get
back to normal.
Now that all the
reporters have left,
the soda counter
seems empty.
Pete's up at

Buzzard Point
probably picking up
more rocks
& dreaming about
being a geologist.
Well . . . rocks are
not my thing—
I *do* love fishing
but I'm not sure
I can make my
living at it.
Reckon I got
all next year
to figure out my
future. (I sure
don't want to
be a lawyer—
too much public
speaking!) But this
Monkey Trial's
made one thing
pretty clear:
it's not easy to
stand by your
beliefs & keep
your mind open
at the same time.
That takes a lot
of practice, a lot

of patience. Just
like baseball . . .

& fishing.

PETER SYKES

The low haze that's been hanging
over these hills for the past two weeks
has finally cleared. Up here, there's

a cool breeze and you can almost hear
the pines sigh in relief. Now that the
trial's ended and my job at Robinson's

is done, I have a little more money
and a lot more time to think. Today I
made a list of things I could buy

with my earnings: a new fishing pole,
wading boots, display cases for my
rocks. I kept changing it. And then I

tore it up. What I really want to do is
take Marybeth out to dinner and to
the movie house at Morgan Springs.

I do think she likes me—I know I
like her a lot (even if, as Jimmy
Lee says, she has a temper).

I plan to tell her about that note
the geologist left me, and how
I might have a future in science.

I plan to ask her what she wants to do
with her future, too, because I think
we might have a lot to talk about

once I ask her out. I know she likes
to watch movies and to read good books.
Lord! I hope she also likes rocks.

CONSTABLE FRAYBEL

I wonder
what those five drugstore conspirators

are thinking now.
Dayton had its visitors, all right,
but most were local Tennessee folks, just like us.
Books and monkey masks
sold well
and so did Robinson's sodas.
But no one in Dayton got rich.

All the same, we witnessed
two of the greatest speakers in America
lock their horns in a battle
that won't soon be forgotten.

I imagine someday
this trial *will* be famous for changing the way
people think about their history,
especially these children.

Just now I saw
a Model T full of young people
heading down the road to Morgan Springs,
and Betty Barker preaching her gospel
to Willy Amos, who looks like he's taken
to reading books
between selling pears and berries;
J. T. Scopes is heading out to the tennis court,
and Jimmy Lee Davis is going fishing
up at Connor's Pond.

Some things will change, some
will stay the same. My job's to make sure
both
take place in peace.

TILLIE STACKHOUSE

Well, I got another hug.
This time it was that young,
good-looking reporter from St. Louis
and it happened right before
he left the Mansion for the station.

He flustered me something awful,
saying he'd never had such good cooking,
such sound sleeping away from home,
and he'd come back sometime
just to visit.

I thanked him again for letting me
and Marybeth sit with him
in court.
"There's no doubt, Mr. Lebrun," I said,
"you've got *very* good instincts."

He asked me (was he kidding?)
if I'd be willing
to put that in writing
for his boss.

BETTY BARKER

I met up with that young reporter
as he was making for the train.
I told him he needed to spread
    the good word
about our Lord's victory here in Dayton
and how Clarence Darrow
and his team of heathens
were silenced by
    the judge's gavel,
    the jury's decision,
    and the judgment of Almighty God.

"Ma'am," he said, "with all due respect,
I'm paid to write what happens
without embellishment."

Embellishment . . . ha! I gave him
a stack of anti-evolution pamphlets

so he could distribute them
where he's from.
"But I'm a Christian
who believes in evolution," he said.

I told that young man
I'd pray for his soul. I gave him a second
stack, put him on the train,

sent him back home
with my blessings.

WILLY AMOS

I offered to take
Clarence Darrow's suitcase to the train.
"That's all right, son," he said.
"I've only got one and it's small, easy to carry."

Then he recognized me.

"Aren't you the young man
who defends evergreens?"
He grinned and scratched underneath his suspenders.

"I hope you'll keep arguing to the trees.
Maybe someday I'll see you in court!"

I nodded, then kicked the dirt.
"I'm colored," I said.

"Yes, I noticed," Mr. Darrow replied.
(These lawyers can be real sharp, they can!)

"Well," I pointed out, "there ain't no such thing
as a colored lawyer."

He looked at me, but not like
he was angry.

"Son," he finally said, "I get paid to ask
the very best questions I can.
And before I board this train, I'm going to
ask one more:
Do you plan to let that
stop you?"

TILLIE STACKHOUSE

Dear Lila:

I've decided to accept your offer
of a week in New York City.
It will be so good to see you again. . . .
We can stay up late talking,
see the sights, go shopping, maybe
even watch those bob-haired dancers
at the Parody Club doing the Charleston.

I'll arrive by train on August 15
and will ring you from the station.
Until then, I plan to spend
any free time I can find
with Darwin's book.
Since the day it came, I've been so busy
cooking and cleaning, I've hardly
had any time to read it!

When I'm through, I hope you won't mind,
but I'll be passing it on
to Marybeth. This trial's lit a fire
in that girl's mind, which was already
quick to begin with.

Who knows . . . when she goes off to college,
she might even leave it
for our dear, stubborn cousin Frank.

And that would surely prove
the idea of evolution!

Your loving sister,
Tillie

ERNEST McMANUS

This was a vacation well spent. Despite
my recent intimacy with some Tennessee
garden bees, I will have
almost nothing but fond memories
of this place,
plus a few nuggets of thought in my journal
that might—with a little time and work—
turn into a few good sermons.

With my leg still a little sore, a middle-
aged Negro offered me a lift
to the station in his wagon.
On the way, I asked him
what he thought about the trial
(I'd seen him there nearly every day
with his teenage son)
and the idea of evolution.
He thought a minute:

"There's good in everyone and there's
evil in everyone," he said.
"An' I believe it's been that way
for as long as there's been men—
seven minutes, seven days, or seven million years."

I thanked him for the lift, tipped him,
and shook his hard-callused hand.
It's strange, I thought, how we look
for wisdom in books,
but just as often it resides
in the man or woman
right beside us.

MARYBETH DODD

"Marybeth! Come on out here, will you?"
The way Daddy said it, I didn't argue.

He sat on the top porch step,
staring at a photograph of Mama,
which he held tight in both hands
like it was something someone might
snatch away.

He didn't look at me when he spoke.
"Your ma always wanted me to take her
to see a big Tennessee city
like Knoxville, Nashville, or Memphis.
I promised her I would. Those early years, though,
we hardly had the money
to take ourselves to Morgan Springs,
let alone any of those other places.
When we finally did have some to spare,
we bought this house here,
so we'd have a nice place to raise you.
Then, when your ma got sick
and we knew she wouldn't get better,
I asked Doc Nichols if we could take a trip
to Knoxville to cheer her up.
Doc said she was too weak. He said
a trip like that might kill her sooner
than the Lord was fixin' to take her."

The photograph was shaking. I put my
hand on his wrist, real gentle, and he
didn't push away.

"Since your ma died, Marybeth, I haven't
thought much about travelin'.
But the older you get, the more you
resemble your mother. She liked books.
She liked adventure and new ideas.
Her nature was to be curious, like you.

So I've been thinkin' . . . maybe you and I
ought to borrow Tillie's jalopy
and head up to Knoxville, maybe
take a tour of the university. . . ."

Poor Daddy. I didn't let him finish.
I think I squeezed his wrist so hard
it almost bled. But as I was
squealing with relief and spinning myself
dizzy around our cherry tree,
I could clearly see

Daddy's big, easy grin spreading across his face
like moon glow on the snow
of a cold, dark Tennessee night.

I think this case will be remembered because it is
the first case of this sort since we stopped trying
people in America for witchcraft.

—Clarence Darrow, defense lawyer

Here has been fought out a little case
of little consequence as a case . . . [But]
the issue will someday be settled right,
whether it is settled on our side or the other side.

—William Jennings Bryan, prosecution lawyer

EPILOGUE: AFTER THE TRIAL

The following is a summary of what happened to the town and to the real historical figures involved in the Dayton case after the trial concluded.

Dayton, Tennessee: The town's economic boom was short-lived. Almost immediately after the verdict was announced, the remaining visitors and journalists packed their bags and went back to their respective cities, towns, and farms. Even the nation's newspapers—which at that time numbered more than 2,300—wrote their final editorials, then promptly dropped the subject of the Dayton trial. One positive outcome, however, was the establishment of William Jennings Bryan University (later shortened to Bryan College). Named for the famous prosecutor who had argued so fervently on behalf of Christian fundamentalism, it began in 1930 and continues today, offering bachelor's degrees in sixteen subject areas.

J. T. Scopes: The experience of being the lone defendant in the most publicized trial of the early 1900s made the shy, intelligent high school math and science teacher question his future. At the conclusion of the Dayton case, several of the expert witnesses who had come to testify on his behalf offered him a scholarship. Impressed by his courage and his enthusiasm for intellectual pursuits, they agreed to pay for his graduate education in any field he chose. Meanwhile, the Rhea County school board offered to extend Scopes's teaching contract into the next year, as long as he promised not to teach evolution. For Scopes, the choice was easy: he enrolled at the University of Chicago and became a geologist.

W. J. Bryan: Despite the jury's ruling in his favor, the trial proved to be a difficult experience for Bryan in several ways. When Darrow put him on the witness stand, he exposed Bryan's extreme lack of knowledge about—as well as his lack of interest in—a world that was moving past him in science and technology. Newspapers across the country mocked Bryan's self-imposed ignorance in their cartoons and editorials. Yet even those who disagreed with his position on biblical literalism admired his steadfast faith. Bryan spent many days preparing his closing arguments, but because of legal technicalities, he never had a chance to deliver them. Upon learning that he would have no grand finale, he was bitterly disappointed.

The intense July heat also took its toll on Bryan, who was overweight and in poor health. Nevertheless, in the days following the trial, Bryan accepted several invitations to speak in nearby towns such as Jasper and Winchester. On the following Sunday, five days after the trial concluded, Bryan died in his sleep, apparently of heart failure. The three-time presidential candidate was buried in Arlington National Cemetery, near the

Capitol. Flags were lowered to half-mast, newspapers printed extended obituaries, and thousands came to mourn his death.

Clarence Darrow: In his early years as a lawyer, Darrow had been motivated by the belief that the justice system treated the poor unfairly and the rich too leniently. In court, he argued against child labor, capital punishment, and racial segregation, and in favor of workers' rights. His belief that socially imposed fears and psychological pressures lay at the root of most crimes made him unpopular with many Americans.

Despite their obvious differences on the evolution issue, Darrow and Bryan had enjoyed a solid friendship in the years preceding the Scopes trial. Darrow had, in fact, campaigned for Bryan when he ran for president. During the trial, however, their differences became too great to overcome and they parted somewhat bitterly. Darrow's book *Crime: Its Cause and Treatment*, published in 1922, solidified his reputation as one of the country's most liberal thinkers. After the Scopes trial, he continued to write and to defend those he felt were unjustly accused. He lived until 1938.

Scopes trial appeal: Roughly a year after the Dayton trial, Darrow and several other defense lawyers appealed the case to the Supreme Court of Tennessee. Of the four judges who heard the case, two upheld the guilty verdict, one upheld the constitutionality of the law (but because the theory of evolution did not deny the Divine Creation, he disagreed with the guilty verdict), and one found the law itself unconstitutional. Therefore, by a three-judge majority ruling, the Butler Act remained in effect in Tennessee until it was repealed in September 1967. The state supreme court did, however, revoke Scopes's $100 fine. The defense team's plan to take the case to the U.S. Supreme Court was also denied on a technicality. All across America the evolution debate continued nonetheless, fueling legal actions that would continue over the next several decades.

The anti-evolution movement: After Bryan's death, his followers continued his fundamentalist campaign, with the goal of having anti-evolution laws passed in as many states as possible. They were successful in only a handful, though, and by the end of the Second World War, the Dayton trial had become merely another episode in legal history. Even so, its lingering impact on public school courses remained evident. In the decades following the Scopes trial, high school textbook editors refrained from including Darwin or evolution, or introduced them only minimally. Teachers, too, became nervous about losing their jobs if they discussed the subject in any depth in their classrooms. Thus, despite the narrow legal impact of the Scopes verdict, its educational impact was measurable and profound.

In the 1960s, the United States became concerned about the increasing scientific and technological advances of other countries (especially the USSR). It was during this time that public opinion shifted again and evolution was less frequently denounced than it had been in the first half of the century. In addition, the immense social changes that occurred during this time made it more acceptable for individuals to have a less rigid stance on the issue. In general, religious leaders and intellectuals alike saw less contradiction between faith and rational science.

Despite this apparent closing of the science/religion gap, there remains today a significant number of Americans who feel that belief in evolution weakens religious faith and that belief in evolution and belief in God are distinct, competing alternatives that are irreconcilable. Many also feel that every science class should include a disclaimer before any mention of evolution is made. So far, in the early twenty-first century, several state courts, including those of Kansas and Pennsylvania, have heard arguments for and against the teaching of evolution and the introduction of the concept of intelligent design into public school science programs. (Proponents of intelligent design argue that certain aspects of life on earth and in the universe are best explained through an "intelligent cause" or a "creator God" and not by natural selection.) From these recent events, it is clear that the Scopes trial legacy has had a much greater impact than any of the original "drugstore conspirators" could have imagined.

AUTHOR'S NOTE

One of the primary duties of a novelist who writes about the past is to remain as historically accurate as possible. In this story, the terms *colored* and *Negro* are used in third-party reference and in self-reference by black characters because that was the norm in 1925. Especially in the southern states, these terms were commonly used—in speech and published writing—until the 1960s. Since then, both designations have become unacceptable and are frequently associated with the oppressive decades preceding the civil rights movement.

You will also notice that Paul Lebrun, the fictional journalist in *Ringside, 1925*, writes in a much more personal, conversational style than most news reporters do today. That this was typical of the time became evident as I read many dozens of newspaper articles in the course of my research. I therefore made every attempt to echo the journalistic style of the 1920s in Lebrun's reports for the *St. Louis Post-Dispatch*.

In addition to the many articles, books, and Web pages I read during my research, I was fortunate to be able to visit the town of Dayton, Tennessee, and to witness the annual Scopes trial reenactment in the Rhea County Courthouse. This experience allowed me to conjure more accurately the impressions and emotions of a typical Dayton citizen both prior to and during the actual historical trial. During my stay, I walked along the same streets that Bryan, Darrow, and Scopes had walked, stood before several of the stores and buildings mentioned in the story (I even exercised inside Rhea County High, which has since been converted to a YMCA), and perused the wonderful exhibits of the Scopes Trial Museum in the basement of the courthouse. It's a journey I highly recommend to anyone wishing to relive the original events of that famous summer, whose core controversies still resonate in the twenty-first century.

—J.B.

To learn more about the Scopes trial and the evolution controversy:

Adler, Jerry. "Charles Darwin: Evolution of a Scientist." *Newsweek*, November 28, 2005.

Caudill, Edward, et al. *The Scopes Trial: A Photographic History*. Knoxville: University of Tennessee Press, 2000.

Inherit the Wind. Directed by Stanley Kramer. MGM Studios, Inc., 1960; MGM Home, 2001.

Israel, Charles A. *Before Scopes: Evangelicalism, Education, and Evolution in Tennessee, 1870–1925*. Athens: University of Georgia Press, 2004.

Kemper, Steve. "Evolution on Trial." *Smithsonian*, April 2005.

Larson, Edward J. *Summer for the Gods*. Cambridge: Harvard University Press, 1997.

Lawrence, Jerome, and Robert E. Lee. *Inherit the Wind*. New York: Bantam Books, 1960, c1955. (1st perf. Jan. 10, 1955).

Linder, Douglas O. "Tennessee vs. John Scopes: The 'Monkey Trial,' 1925." *Famous Trials in American History*. 2002. www.law.umkc.edu/faculty/projects/ftrials/scopes/scopes.htm

Moran, Jeffrey P. *The Scopes Trial: A Brief History with Documents*. Bedford Series in History and Culture. New York: Bedford/ St. Martin's, 2002.

Wallis, Claudia. "The Evolution Wars." *Time*, August 15, 2005.

www.tnhistoryforkids.org/places/scopes_museum

ACKNOWLEDGMENTS

My sincere thanks to the following people and institutions, who contributed their wisdom, knowledge, and encouragement during the writing of this book:

Joan Slattery, senior executive editor at Knopf/Crown Books for Young Readers; Allison Wortche, assistant editor at Knopf/Crown; the reference staff at the Chester County Library, Exton, Pennsylvania; Janet Williams, associate professor of biology at Elms College; the town of Dayton, Tennessee, and in particular the Scopes trial reenactors; the Scopes Trial Museum in Dayton; Susan Brennan, reading specialist; my husband, Neil, and my daughter, Leigh, whose patience and support remained unwavering throughout the long haul of this project.

Also by Jen Bryant

Pieces of Georgia

★ "Through Georgia's artwork, noticing details others miss, learning about painters like O'Keeffe and Wyeth, and reaching out to others, the fragmented pieces of this steely, gentle heroine become an integrated whole."—*Publishers Weekly*, Starred

"A remarkable book. . . . The finely drawn characters come to life. . . . Their story is a universal one of love, friendship, and loss and will be appreciated by a wide audience."
—*School Library Journal*

A *Voice of Youth Advocates* Top Shelf Fiction for Middle School Readers Selection
An NCSS-CBC Notable Social Studies Trade Book for Young People

The Trial

★ "Extraordinary. . . . As Katie says, 'When a man's on trial for his life/isn't *every* word important?' Bryant shows why with art and humanity."—*Booklist*, Starred

"Bryant crafts a memorable heroine and unfolds a thought-provoking tale."
—*Publishers Weekly*

"Readers . . . will be swept along in suspense."—*The Horn Book Magazine*

A Book Sense 76 Pick
A Bank Street College of Education Best Children's Book of the Year

Also by Jen Bryant

Kaleidoscope Eyes

When Lyza helps her dad clean out her late Gramps's house, a mysterious surprise brightens the sad task. In her grandfather's dusty attic, Lyza discovers three maps, carefully folded and stacked, bound by a single rubber band. On top, an envelope says, "For Lyza ONLY." What could this possibly be? With the help of her two best friends and a cryptic letter from Gramps, Lyza uncovers an impossible mystery: a three-hundred-year-old pirate treasure might actually be buried in her own New Jersey town. And Lyza, Malcolm, and Carolann alone hold the clues, if only they can decipher them. Can three thirteen-year-olds actually conduct a secret treasure hunt? And what will they find?

The year is 1968, and sleepless nights, grueling digs, and broken curfews are hardly the only strains on Lyza and her friends: their town is slowly losing its boys and men to war. Inspired by a true story of buried treasure, Jen Bryant weaves an emotional and suspenseful novel in poems set in the shadow of the Vietnam War during a pivotal year in U.S. history.